Griffith Gaunt

Or, Jealousy

Vol. II

By

Charles Reade

Double 9 BOOKS

Griffith Gaunt

Or, Jealousy

Vol. II

by Charles Reade

ISBN: 978-93-61424-88-5

Published by

DOUBLE 9 BOOKS

2/13-B, Ansari Road
Darvaganj, New Delhi – 110002
info@double9books.com
www.double9books.com
Tel. 011-40042856

ABOUT THE AUTHOR

Charles Reade, a British novelist and dramatist, is best known for his work The Cloister and the Hearth. Charles Reade was born in Ipsden, Oxfordshire, to John Reade and Anne Marie Scott-Waring. He had at least four brothers. He received his B.A. from Magdalen College, Oxford, in 1835, and later became a fellow of the college. He then became dean of arts and vice-president, and in 1847 he received his D.C.L degree. His name was entered at Lincoln's Inn in 1836; he was chosen a Vinerian Fellow in 1842 and admitted to the bar in 1843. He maintained his fellowship at Magdalen throughout his life, but after receiving his degree, he spent the majority of his time in London. William Winwood Reade, the prominent historian, was his nephew. Reade began his writing career as a dramatist, and he elected to list "dramatist" first on his tombstone. As an author, he was always aware of the stage effect in scenes, settings, and conversation. His first comedy, The Ladies' Battle, debuted at the Olympic Theatre in May 1851. It was succeeded by Angela (1851), A Village Tale (1852), The Lost Husband (1852), and Gold (1853).

CONTENTS

CHAPTER I

One day, at dinner, Father Francis let them know that he was ordered to another part of the county, and should no longer be able to enjoy their hospitality. "I am sorry for it," said Griffith, heartily; and Mrs. Gaunt echoed him out of politeness; but, when husband and wife came to talk it over in private, she let out all of a sudden, and for the first time, that the spiritual coldness of her governor had been a great misfortune to her all these years. "His mind," said she, "is set on earthly things. Instead of helping the angels to raise my thoughts to heaven, and heavenly things, he drags me down to earth. Oh, that man's soul was born without wings."

Griffith ventured to suggest that Francis was, nevertheless, an honest man, and no mischief-maker.

Mrs. Gaunt soon disposed of this. "Oh, there are plenty of honest men in the world," said she; "but in one's spiritual director, one needs something more than that, and I have pined for it like a thirsty soul in the desert all these years. Poor good man, I love him dearly; but, thank heaven, he is going."

The next time Francis came, Mrs. Gaunt took an opportunity to inquire, but in the most delicate way, who was to be his successor.

"Well," said he, "I fear you will have no one for the present: I mean no one very fit to direct you in practical matters; but in all that tends directly to the welfare of the soul you will have one young in years but old in good works, and very much my superior in piety."

"I think you do yourself injustice, father," said Mrs. Gaunt, sweetly. She was always polite; and, to be always polite, you must be sometimes insincere.

"No, my daughter," said Father Francis, quietly, "thank God, I know my own defects, and they teach me a little humility. I discharge my religious duties punctually, and find them wholesome and composing; but I lack that holy unction, that spiritual imagination, by which more favoured Christians have fitted themselves to converse with angels. I have too much body, I suppose, and too little soul. I own to you that I cannot look, forward to the hour of death as a happy release from the burden of the flesh. Life is pleasant to me; immortality tempts me not; the pure in heart delight me; but in the sentimental part of religion I feel myself dry and barren. I fear God, and desire to do His will; but I cannot love Him as the saints have done; my spirit is too dull, too gross. I have often been unable to keep pace with you in your pious and lofty aspirations: and this softens my regret at quitting you; for you will be in better hands, my daughter."

Mrs. Gaunt was touched by her old friend's humility, and gave him both hands, with the tears in her eyes. But she said nothing; the subject was delicate; and really she could not honestly contradict him.

A day or two afterwards he brought his successor to the house; a man so remarkable that Mrs. Gaunt almost started at first sight of him. Born of an Italian mother, his skin was dark, and his eyes coal black; yet his ample but symmetrical forehead was singularly white and delicate. Very tall and spare, and both face and figure were of that exalted kind which make ordinary beauty seem dross. In short, he was one of those ethereal priests the Roman Catholic Church produces every now and then by way of incredible contrast to the thickset peasants in black that form her staple. This Brother Leonard looked and moved like a being who had come down from some higher sphere to pay the world a very little visit, and be very kind and patient with it all the time.

He was presented to Mrs. Gaunt, and bowed calmly, coldly, and with a certain mixture of humility and superiority, and gave her but one tranquil glance, then turned his eyes inward as before.

Mrs. Gaunt, on the contrary, was almost fluttered at being presented so suddenly to one who seemed to her Religion embodied. She blushed, and looked timidly at him, and was anxious not to make an unfavourable impression.

She found it, however, very difficult to make any impression at all. Leonard had no small talk, and met her advances in that line with courteous monosyllables; and when she, upon this, turned and chatted with Father Francis, he did not wait for an opening to strike in, but sought a shelter from her commonplaces in his own thoughts.

Then Mrs. Gaunt yielded to her genuine impulse, and began to talk about the prospects of the Church, and what might be done to reconvert the British Isles to the true faith. Her cheek flushed, and her eye shone with the theme; and Francis smiled paternally: but the young priest drew back; Mrs. Gaunt saw in a moment that he disapproved of a woman meddling with so high a matter uninvited. If he had said so she had spirit enough to have resisted; but the cold, lofty look of polite but grave disapproval, dashed her courage and reduced her to silence.

She soon recovered so far as to be piqued. She gave her whole attention to Francis, and, on parting with her guests, she curtsied coldly to Leonard, and said to Francis, "Ah, my dear friend, I foresee I shall miss you terribly."

I am afraid this pretty speech was intended as a side cut at Leonard.

But on the impassive ice the lightnings play.

Her new confessor retired, and left her with a sense of inferiority, which would have been pleasing to her woman's nature, if Leonard himself had appeared less conscious of it, and had shown ever so little approval of herself; but, impressed upon her too sharply, it piqued and mortified her.

However, like a gallant champion, she awaited another encounter. She so rarely failed to please, she could not accept defeat.

Father Francis departed.

Mrs. Gaunt soon found that she really missed him. She had got into a habit of running to her confessor twice a week, and to her director nearly every day that he did not come of his own accord to her.

Her good sense showed her at once she must not take up Brother Leonard's time in this way. She went a long while, for her, without confession: at last she sent a line to Leonard asking him when it would be convenient to him to confess her. Leonard wrote back to say that he received penitents in the chapel for two hours after matins every Monday, Tuesday, and Saturday.

This implied first come, first served; and was rather galling to Mrs. Gaunt.

However, she rode one morning, with her groom behind her, and had to wait until an old woman in a red cloak and black bonnet was first disposed of. She confessed a heap. And presently the soft but chill tones of Brother Leonard broke in with these freezing words: "My daughter, excuse me; but confession is one thing, gossip about ourselves is another."

This distinction was fine, but fatal. The next minute the fair penitent was in her carriage, her eyes filled with tears of mortification.

"The man is a spiritual machine," said she; and her pride was mortified to the core.

In these happy days she used to open her heart to her husband; and she went so far as to say some bitter little feminine things of her new confessor, before him.

He took no notice at first; but at last he said one day, "Well, I am of your mind; he is very poor company compared with that jovial old blade, Francis.

But why so many words, Kate? You don't use to bite twice at a cherry: if the milksop is not to your taste, give him the sack and be hanged to him." And with this homely advice Squire Gaunt dismissed the matter and went to the stable to give his mare a ball.

So you see Mrs. Gaunt was discontented with Francis for not being an enthusiast, and nettled with Leonard for being one.

The very next Sunday morning she went and heard Leonard preach. His first sermon was an era in her life. After twenty years of pulpit prosers, there suddenly rose before her a sacred orator; an orator born; blest with that divine and thrilling eloquence that no heart can really resist. He prepared his great theme with art at first; but, once warm, it carried him away and his hearers went with him like so many straws on the flood. And in the exercise of this great gift the whole man seemed transfigured; abroad, he was a languid, rather slouching priest, who crept about, a picture of delicate humility, but with a shade of meanness; for, religious prejudice apart, it is ignoble to sweep the wall in passing as he did, and eye the ground; but, once in the pulpit, his figure rose and swelled majestically, and seemed to fly over them all like a guardian angel's; his sallow cheek burned, his great Italian eye shot black lightning at the impenitent, and melted ineffably when he soothed the sorrowful.

Observe that great, mean, brown bird in the Zoological Gardens, which sits so tame on its perch, and droops and slouches like a drowsy duck. That is the great and soaring eagle. Who would believe it, to look at him? Yet all he wants is to be put in his right place instead of his wrong. He is not himself in man's cages, belonging to God's sky. Even so Leonard was abroad in the world, but at home in the pulpit: and so he somewhat crept and slouched about the parish; but soared like an eagle in his native air.

Mrs. Gaunt sat thrilled, enraptured, melted. She hung upon his words; and, when they ceased, she still sat motionless, spell-bound; loath to believe that accents so divine could really come to an end.

Even, whilst all the rest were dispersing, she sat quite still, and closed her eyes. For her soul was too high-strung now to endure the chit-chat she knew would attack her on the road home—chit-chat that had been welcome enough, coming home from other preachers.

And by this means she came hot and undiluted to her husband; she laid her white hand on his shoulder, and said, "Oh, Griffith, I have heard the voice of God."

Griffith looked alarmed, and rather shocked than elated.

Mrs. Gaunt observed that, and tacked on, "Speaking by the lips of his servant." But she fired again the next moment, and said, "The grave hath given us back St. Paul in the Church's need; and I have heard him this day."

"Good heavens! where?"

"At St. Mary's Chapel."

Then Griffith looked very incredulous. Then she gushed out with, "What, because it is a small chapel, you think a great saint cannot be in it. Why, our Saviour was born in a stable, if you go to that."

"Well, but my dear, consider," said Griffith; "who ever heard of comparing a living man to St. Paul, for preaching? Why, he was an apostle, for one thing; and there are no apostles nowadays. He made Felix tremble on his throne, and almost persuaded Whatsename, another heathen gentleman, to be a Christian."

"That is true," said the lady, thoughtfully; "but he sent one man that *we* know of to sleep. Catch Brother Leonard sending any man to sleep! And then nobody will ever say of *him* that he was long preaching."

"Why, I do say it," replied Griffith. "By the same token, I have been waiting dinner for you this half-hour, along of his preaching."

"Ah, that's because you did not hear him," retorted Mrs. Gaunt: "if you had, it would have seemed too short, and you would have forgotten all about your dinner for once."

Griffith made no reply, He even looked vexed at her enthusiastic admiration. She saw, and said no more. But after dinner she retired to the grove, and thought of the sermon and the preacher: thought of them all the more that she was discouraged from enlarging on them. And it would have been kinder, and also wiser, of Griffith, if he had encouraged her to let out her heart to him on this subject, although it did not happen to interest him. A husband should not chill an enthusiastic wife, and, above all, should never separate himself from her favourite topic, when she loves him well enough to try and share it with him.

Mrs. Gaunt, however, though her feelings were quick, was not cursed with a sickly or irritable sensibility; nor, on the other hand, was she one of those lovely little bores who cannot keep their tongues off their favourite theme. She quietly let the subject drop for a whole week; but the next Sunday morning she asked her husband if he would do her a little favour.

"I'm more likely to say ay than nay," was the cheerful reply.

"It is just to go to chapel with me; and then you can judge for yourself."

Griffith looked rather sheepish at this proposal; and said he could not very well do that.

"Why not, dearest, just for once?"

"Well, you see, parties run so high in this parish; and everything one does is noted. Why, if I was to go to chapel, they'd say directly, 'Look at Griffith Gaunt: he is so tied to his wife's apron he is going to give up the faith of his ancestors.'"

"The faith of your ancestors! That is a good jest. The faith of your grandfather at the outside: the faith of your ancestors was the faith of mine and me."

"Well, don't let us differ about a word," said Griffith; "you know what I mean. Did ever I ask you to go to church with me? and, if I were to ask you, would you go?"

Mrs. Gaunt coloured; but would not give in. "That is not the same thing," said she. "I do profess religion: you do not. You scarce think of God on week days; and, indeed, never mention his name except in the way of swearing; and on Sunday you go to church—for what? to doze before dinner, you know you do. Come now, with you 'tis no question of religion, but just of nap or no nap: for Brother Leonard won't let you sleep, I warn you fairly."

Griffith shook his head. "You are too hard on me, wife. I know I am not so good as you are, and never shall be; but that is not the fault of the Protestant faith, which hath reared so many holy men: and some of 'em our *ancestors* burnt alive, and will burn in hell themselves for the deed. But, look you, sweetheart, if I'm not a saint I'm a gentleman, and, say I wear my faith loose, I won't drag it in the dirt none the more for that. So you must excuse me."

Mrs. Gaunt was staggered; and, if Griffith had said no more, I think she would have withdrawn her request, and so the matter ended. But persons unversed in argument can seldom let well alone; and this simple squire must needs go on to say, "Besides, Kate, it would come to the parson's ears, and he is a friend of mine, you know. Why, I shall be sure to meet him to-morrow."

"Ay," retorted the lady, "by the cover-side. Well, when you do, tell him you refused your wife your company for fear of offending the religious views of a fox-hunting parson."

"Nay, Kate," said Griffith, "this is not to ask thy man to go with thee: 'tis to say go he must, willy nilly." With that he rose and rang the bell. "Order the chariot," said he, "I am to go with our dame."

Mrs. Gaunt's face beamed with gratified pride and affection. The chariot came round, and Griffith handed his dame in. He then gave an involuntary sigh, and followed her with a hang-dog look.

She heard the sigh, and saw the look, and laid her hand quickly on his shoulder, and said, gently but coldly, "Stay you at home, my dear. We shall meet at dinner."

"As you will," said he, cheerfully: and they went their several ways. He congratulated himself on her clemency, and his own escape. She went along, sorrowful at having to drink so great a bliss alone; and thought it unkind and stupid of Griffith not to yield with a good grace if he could yield at all; and, indeed, women seem cleverer than men in this, that, when they resign their wills, they do it graciously and not by halves. Perhaps they are more accustomed to knock under; and you know practice makes perfect.

But every smaller feeling was swept away by the preacher, and Mrs. Gaunt came home full of pious and lofty thoughts.

She found her husband seated at the dinner-table, with one turnip before him; and even that was not comestible; for it was his grandfather's watch, with a face about the size of a new-born child's. "Forty-five minutes past one, Kate," said he, ruefully.

"Well, why not bid them serve the dinner?" said she, with an air of consummate indifference.

"What, dine alone o' Sunday? Why, you know I couldn't eat a morsel without you, set opposite."

Mrs. Gaunt smiled affectionately. "Well, then, my dear, we had better order dinner an hour later next Sunday."

"But that will upset the servants, and spoil their Sunday."

"And am I to be their slave?" said Mrs. Gaunt, getting a little warm. "Dinner! dinner! What! shall I starve my soul, by hurrying away from the oracles of God to a sirloin? Oh, these gross appetites! how they deaden the immortal half, and wall out Heaven's music! For my part, I wish there was no such thing as eating and drinking; 'tis like falling from Heaven down into the mud, to come back from such divine discourse and be greeted with 'dinner! dinner! dinner!'"

The next Sunday, after waiting half an hour for her, Griffith began, his dinner without her.

And this time, on her arrival, instead of remonstrating with her, he excused himself. "Nothing," said he, "upsets a man's temper like waiting for his dinner."

"Well, but you have not waited."

"Yes, I did, a good half-hour. Till I could wait no longer."

"Well, dear, if I were you I would not have waited at all, or else waited till your wife came home."

"Ah, dame, that is all very well for you to say. You could live on hearing of sermons and smelling to rosebuds. You don't know what 'tis to be a hungry man."

The next Sunday he sat sadly down, and finished his dinner without her. And she came home and sat down to half-empty dishes; and ate much less than she used when she had him to keep her company in it.

Griffith, looking on disconsolate, told her she was more like a bird pecking, than a Christian eating of a Sunday.

"No matter, child," said she; "so long as my soul is filled with the bread of Heaven."

Leonard's eloquence suffered no diminution, either in quantity or quality, and, after a while, Gaunt gave up his rule of never dining abroad on the Sunday. If his wife was not punctual, his stomach was: and he had not the same temptation to dine at home he used to have.

And, indeed, by degrees, instead of quietly enjoying his wife's company on that sweet day, he got to see less of her than on the week days.

CHAPTER II

Your mechanical preacher flings his words out happy-go-lucky; but the pulpit orator, like every other orator, feels his people's pulse as he speaks, and vibrates with them, and they with him.

So Leonard soon discovered he had a great listener in Mrs. Gaunt: she was always there whenever he preached, and her rapt attention never flagged. Her grey eyes never left his face, and, being up-turned, the full orbs came out in all their grandeur, and seemed an angel's come down from Heaven to hear him: for, indeed, to a very dark man, as Leonard was, the gentle radiance of a true Saxon beauty seems always more or less angelic.

By degrees this face became a help to the orator. In preaching he looked sometimes to it for sympathy, and lo, it was sure to be melting with sympathy. Was he led on to higher or deeper thoughts than most of his congregation could understand, he looked to this face to understand him; and lo, it had quite understood him, and was beaming with intelligence.

From a help and an encouragement it became a comfort and a delight to him.

On leaving the pulpit and cooling, he remembered its owner was no angel, but a woman of the world, and had put to him frivolous questions.

The illusion, however, was so beautiful that Leonard, being an imaginative man, was unwilling to dispel it by coming into familiar contact with Mrs. Gaunt. So he used to make his assistant visit her, and receive her when she came to confess, which was very rarely; for she was discouraged by her first reception.

Brother Leonard lived in a sort of dwarf monastery, consisting of two cottages, an oratory, and a sepulchre. The two latter were old, but the cottages had been built expressly for him and another seminary priest who had been invited from France. Inside, these cottages were little more than cells; only the bigger had a kitchen, which was a glorious place compared with the parlour: for it was illuminated with bright pewter plates, copper vessels, brass candlesticks, and a nice clean woman, with a plain gown kilted over a quilted silk petticoat; Betty Scarf, an old servant of Mrs. Gaunt's, who had married, and was now the widow Gough.

She stood at the gate one day as Mrs. Gaunt drove by; and curtsied, all beaming.

Mrs. Gaunt stopped the carriage, and made some kind and patronizing inquires about her: and it ended in Betty asking her to come in and see her place. Mrs. Gaunt looked a little shy at that, and did not move. "Nay, they are both abroad till supper time," said Betty, reading her in a moment by the light of sex. Then Mrs. Gaunt smiled, and got out of her carriage. Betty took her in and showed her everything in doors and out. Mrs. Gaunt looked mighty demure and dignified, but scanned everything closely, only without seeming too curious.

The cold gloom of the parlour struck her. She shuddered, and said, "This would give me the vapours. But, doubtless, angels come and brighten it for *him.*"

"Not always," said Betty. "I do see him with his head in his hand by the hour, and hear him sigh ever so loud as I pass the door. Why, one day he was fain to have me and my spinning wheel aside him. Says he, 'Let me hear thy busy wheel, and see thee ply it.' 'And welcome,' says I. So I sat in his room, and span, and he sat a gloating of me as if he had never seen a woman spin hemp afore (he is a very simple man): and presently says he—but what signifies what he said?"

"Nay, Betty; if you please. I am much interested in him. He preaches so divinely."

"Ay," said Betty, "that's his gift. But a poor trencher-man; and I declare I'm ashamed to eat all the vittels that are eaten here, and me but a woman."

"But what did he say to you that time?" asked Mrs. Gaunt, a little impatiently.

Betty cudgelled her memory. "Well says he, 'My daughter,' (the poor soul always calls me his daughter, and me old enough to be his mother mostly;) says he, 'how comes it that you are never wearied, nor cast down, and yet you but serve a sinner like yourself; but I do often droop in my Master's service, and he is the lord of Heaven and Earth?' Says I, 'I'll tell ye, sir: because ye don't eat enough o' vittels.'"

"What an answer!"

"Why 'tis the truth, dame. And says I, 'If I was to be always fasting, like as you be, d'ye think I should have the heart to work from morn till night?' Now, wasn't I right?"

"I don't know till I hear what answer he made," said Mrs. Gaunt, with mean caution.

"Oh, he shook his head, and said he ate mortal food enow (poor simple body!), but drank too little of grace divine. That was his word."

Mrs. Gaunt was a good deal struck and affected by this revelation, and astonished at the slighting tone Betty took in speaking of so remarkable a man. The saying that "No man is a hero to his valet" was not yet current, or perhaps she would have been less surprised at that.

"Alas! poor man," said she, "and is it so? To hear him, I thought his soul was borne up night and day by angels' pinions—"

The widow interrupted her. "Ay, you hear him preach, and it is like God's trumpet mostly, and so much I say for him in all companies. But I see him directly after; he totters into this very room, and sits him down pale and panting, and one time like to swoon, and another all for crying, and then he is ever so dull and sad for the whole afternoon."

"And nobody knows this but you? You have got my old petticoat still, I see. I must look you up another."

"You are very good, dame, I am sure. 'Twill not come amiss; I've only this for Sundays and all. No, my lady, not a soul but me and you; I'm not one as tells tales out of doors: but I don't mind you, dame; you are my old mistress, and a discreet woman. 'Twill go no further than your ear."

Mrs. Gaunt told her she might rely on that. The widow then inquired after Mrs. Gaunt's little girl, and admired her dress, and described her own ailments, and poured out a continuous stream of topics bearing no affinity to each other except that they were all of them not worth mentioning. And all the while she thus discoursed, Mrs. Gaunt's thoughtful eyes looked straight over the chatterbox's white cap, and explored vacancy: and by-and-by she broke the current of twaddle with the air of a camelopard marching across a running gutter.

"Betsy Gough," said she, "I am thinking."

Mrs. Gough was struck dumb by an announcement so singular.

"I have heard, and I have read, that great and pious and learned men are often to seek in little simple things, such as plain bodies have at their fingers' ends. So now, if you and I could only teach him something for all he has taught us. And, to be sure, we ought to be kind to him if we can; for oh, Betty, my woman, 'tis a poor vanity to go and despise the great, and the learned, and the sainted, because forsooth we find them out in some one little weakness, we that are all made up of weaknesses and defects. So, now, I sit me down in this very chair: so. And sit you there. Now let us, you and me, look at his room quietly, all over, and see what is wanting."

"First and foremost methinks this window should be filled with geraniums; and jessamine; and so forth. With all his learning perhaps he has to be taught, the colour of flowers and golden green leaves, with the sun shining through, how it soothes the eye and relieves the spirits; yet every woman born knows that. Then do but see this bare table! a purple cloth on that, I say."

"Which he will fling it out of the window, I say."

"Nay: for I'll embroider a cross in the middle with gold braid. Then a rose-coloured blind would not be amiss; and there must be a good mirror facing the window; but indeed, if I had my way, I'd paint these horrid walls the first thing."

"How you run on, dame! Bless your heart, you'd turn his den into a palace: he won't suffer that; he is all for self-mortification, poor simple soul."

"Oh, not all at once, I did not mean," said Mrs. Gaunt; "but by little and little, you know. We must begin with the flowers: God made them; and so to be sure he will not spurn *them.*"

Betty began to enter into the plot. "Ay, ay," said she: "the flowers first; and so creep on. But nought will avail to make a man of him so long as he eats but of eggs and garden-stuff, like the beasts of the field, 'that to-day are, and to-morrow are cast into the oven.'"

Mrs. Gaunt smiled at this ambitious attempt of the widow to apply Scripture. Then she said, rather timidly, "Could you make his eggs into omelets? and so pound in a little meat with your small herbs; I dare say he would be none the wiser, and he so bent on high and heavenly things."

"You may take your oath of that."

"Well, then. And I shall send you some stock from the castle, and you can cook his vegetables in good strong gravy, unbeknown."

The widow Gough chuckled aloud.

"But stay," said Mrs. Gaunt; "for us to play the woman so, and delude a saint for his mere bodily weal—will it not be a sin, and a sacrilege to boot?"

"Let that flea stick in the wall," said Betty, contemptuously. "Find you the meat, and I'll find the deceit: for he is as poor as a rat into the bargain. Nay, nay, God Almighty will never have the heart to burn us two for such a trifle. Why, 'tis no more than cheating a froward child taking's physic."

Mrs. Gaunt got into her carriage and went home, thinking all the way. What she had heard filled her with feelings strangely but sweetly composed of veneration and pity. In that Leonard was a great orator and a high-minded priest, she revered him; in that he was solitary and sad, she pitied him; in that he wanted common sense, she felt like a mother, and must take him under her wing. All true women love to protect; perhaps it is a part of the great maternal element; but to protect a man, and yet look up to him, this is delicious.

Leonard, in truth, was one of those high-strung men who pay for their periods of religious rapture by hours of melancholy. This oscillation of the spirits in extraordinary men appears to be more or less a law of nature; and this the widow Gough was not aware of.

The very next Sunday, while he was preaching, she and Mrs. Gaunt's gardener were filling his bow window with flowerpots, the flowers in full bloom and leaf. The said window was large, and had a broad sill outside, and, inside, one of the old fashioned high window-seats that follow the shape of the window. Mrs. Gaunt, who did nothing by halves, sent up a cartload of flowerpots, and Betty and the gardener arranged at least eighty of them, small and great, inside and outside the window.

When Leonard returned from preaching, Betty was at the door to watch. He came past the window with his hands on his breast, and his eyes on the ground, and never saw the flowers in his own window. Betty was disgusted. However, she followed him stealthily as he went to his room, and she heard a profound "Ah!" burst from him.

She bustled in and found him standing in a rapture, with the blood mantling in his pale cheeks, and his dark eyes glowing.

"Now blessed be the heart that hath conceived this thing, and the hand that hath done it," said he. "My poor room it is a bower of roses, all beauty and fragrance." And he sat down inhaling them, and looking at them; and a dreamy, tender complacency crept over his heart, and softened his noble features exquisitely.

Widow Gough, red with gratified pride, stood watching him, and admiring him; but, indeed, she often admired him, though she had got into a way of decrying him.

But at last she lost patience at his want of curiosity; that being a defect she was free from herself. "Ye don't ask me who sent them," said she, reproachfully.

"Nay, nay," said he; "prithee do not tell me: let me divine."

"Divine then," said Betty, roughly. "Which I suppose you means 'guess.'"

"Nay, but let me be quiet awhile," said he, imploringly; "let me sit down and fancy that I am a holy man, and some angel hath turned my cave into a Paradise."

"No more an angel than I am," said the practical widow. "But, now I think on't, y'are not to know who 'twas. Them as sent them they bade me hold my tongue."

This was not true; but Betty, being herself given to unwise revelations and superfluous secresy, chose suddenly to assume that this business was to be clandestine.

The priest turned his eye inwards and meditated. "I see who it is," said he, with an air of absolute conviction. "It must be the lady who comes always when I preach, and her face like none other; it beams with divine intelligence. I will make her all the return we poor priests can make to our benefactors. I will pray for her soul here among the flowers God has made, and she has given his servant to glorify his dwelling. My daughter, you may retire."

This last with surprising, gentle dignity: so Betty went off rather abashed, and avenged herself by adulterating the holy man's innutritions food with Mrs. Gaunt's good gravy; while he prayed fervently for her eternal weal among the flowers she had given him.

Now Mrs. Gaunt, after eight years of married life, was too sensible and dignified a woman to make a romantic mystery out of nothing. She concealed the gravy, because there secresy was necessary; but she never dreamed of hiding that she had sent her spiritual adviser a load of flowers. She did not tell her neighbors, for she was not ostentatious; but she told her husband; who grunted, but did not object.

But Betty's nonsense lent an air of romance and mystery that was well adapted to captivate the imagination of a young, ardent, and solitary spirit like Leonard.

He would have called on the lady he suspected, and thanked her for her kindness. But this he feared would be unwelcome, since she chose to be his unknown benefactress. It would be ill taste in him to tell her he had found her out: it might offend her sensibility, and then she would draw in.

He kept his gratitude therefore to himself, and did not cool it by utterance. He often sat among the flowers, in a sweet reverie, enjoying their color and fragrance: and sometimes he would shut his eyes, and call up the angelical face with great celestial up-turned orbs, and fancy it among her own flowers, and the queen of them all.

These day-dreams did not at that time interfere with his religious duties. They only took the place of those occasional hours, when, partly by the reaction consequent on great religious fervour, partly through exhaustion of the body weakened by fasts, partly by the natural delicacy of his fibre, and the tenderness of his disposition, his soul used to be sad.

By-and-by these languid hours, sad no longer, became sweet and dear to him. He had something so interesting to think of, to dream about. He had a Madonna that cared for him in secret.

She was human; but good, beautiful, and wise. She came to his sermons, and understood every word.

"And she knows me better than I know myself," said he: "since I had these flowers from her hand, I am another man."

One day he came into his room and found two watering pots there. One was large and had a rose to it, the other small and with a plain spout.

"Ah!" said he; and colored with delight. He called Betty, and asked her who had brought them.

"How should I know?" said she, roughly. "I dare say they dropped from Heaven. See, there is a cross painted on 'em in gold letters."

"And so there is!" said Leonard, and crossed himself.

"That means nobody is to use them but you, I trow," said Betty, rather crossly.

The priest's cheek coloured high. "I will use them this instant," said he. "I will revive my drooping children, as they have revived me." And he caught up a watering pot with ardour.

"What, with the sun hot upon 'em?" screamed Betty. "Well, saving your presence, you are a simple man."

"Why, good Betty, 'tis the sun that makes them faint," objected the priest, timidly, and with the utmost humility of manner, though Betty's tone would have irritated a smaller mind.

"Well, well," said she, softening; "but ye see it never rains with a hot sun, and the flowers they know that, and look to be watered after Nature, or else they take it amiss. You, and all your sort, sir, you think to be stronger than nature; you do fast and pray all day, and won't look a woman in the face like other men; and now you wants to water the very flowers at noon."

"Betty," said Leonard, smiling, "I yield to thy superior wisdom, and I will water them at morn and eve. In truth we have all much to learn: let us try and teach one another as kindly as we can."

"I wish you'd teach me to be as humble as you be," blurted out Betty, with something very like a sob: "and more respectful to my betters," added she, angrily.

Watering the flowers she had given him became a solace and a delight to the solitary priest: he always watered them with his own hands and felt quite paternal over them.

One evening Mrs. Gaunt rode by with Griffith and saw him watering them. His tall figure, graceful, though inclined to stoop, bent over them with feminine delicacy, and the simple act, which would have been nothing in vulgar hands, seemed to Mrs. Gaunt so earnest, tender, and delicate in him, that her eyes filled, and she murmured, "Poor Brother Leonard."

"Why, what's wrong with him now?" asked Griffith, a little peevishly.

"That was him watering his flowers."

"Oh, is that all?" said Griffith, carelessly.

Leonard said to himself, "I go too little abroad among my people." He made a little round, and it ended in Hernshaw Castle.

Mrs. Gaunt was out.

He looked disappointed; so the servant suggested that perhaps she was in the Dame's Haunt: he pointed to the grove.

Leonard followed his direction, and soon found himself, for the first time, in that sombre, solemn retreat.

It was a hot summer day, and the grove was delicious. It was also a place well suited to the imaginative and religious mind of the Italian.

He walked slowly to and fro, in religious meditation. Indeed he had nearly thought out his next sermon, when his meditative eye happened to fall on a terrestrial object that startled and thrilled him. Yet it was only a lady's glove. It lay at the foot of a rude wooden seat beneath a gigantic pine.

He stooped and picked it up. He opened the little fingers, and called up in fancy the white and tapering hand that glove could lit. He laid the glove softly on his own palm, and eyed it with dreamy tenderness. "So this is the hand that hath solaced my loneliness," said he: "a hand fair as that angelical face, and sweet as the kind heart that doeth good by stealth."

Then, forgetting for a moment, as lofty spirits will, the difference between meum and tuum, he put the little glove in his bosom, and paced thoughtfully home through the woods, that were separated from the grove only by one meadow: and so he missed the owner of the glove; for she had returned home while he was meditating in her favourite haunt.

Leonard, amongst his other accomplishments, could draw and paint with no mean skill. In one of those hours that used to be of melancholy, but now were hours of dreamy complacency, he took out his pencils and endeavoured to sketch the inspired face that he had learned to preach to, and now to dwell on with gratitude.

Clearly as he saw it before him, he could not reproduce it to his own satisfaction.

After many failures he got very near the mark: yet still something was wanting.

Then, as a last resource, he actually took his sketch to church with him, and in preaching made certain pauses, and, with a very few touches, perfected the likeness; then, on his return home, threw himself on his knees and prayed forgiveness of God with many sighs and tears, and hid the sacrilegious drawing out of his own sight.

Two days after, he was at work colouring it; and the hours flew by like minutes, as he laid the mellow, melting tints on with infinite care and delicacy. Labor ipse voluptas.

Mrs. Gaunt heard Leonard had called on her in person. She was pleased at that, and it encouraged her to carry out her whole design.

Accordingly, one afternoon when she knew Leonard would be at vespers, she sent on a loaded pony-cart, and followed it on horseback.

Then it was all hurry scurry with Betty and her, to get their dark deeds done before their victim's return.

These good creatures set the mirror opposite the flowery window, and so made the room a very bower. They fixed a magnificent crucifix of ivory and gold over the mantelpiece, and they took away his hassock of rashes and substituted a prie-dieu of rich crimson velvet. All that remained was to put their blue cover, with its golden cross, on the table. To do this, however, they had to remove the priest's papers and things: they were covered with a baize cloth. Mrs. Gaunt felt them under it.

"But perhaps he will be angry if we move his papers," said she.

"Not he," said Betty. "He has no secrets from God or man."

"Well, *I* won't take it on me," said Mrs. Gaunt, merrily. "I leave that to you." And she turned her back and settled the mirror, officiously, leaving all the other responsibilities to Betty.

The sturdy widow laughed at her scruples, and whipped off the clot without ceremony. But soon her laugh stopped mighty short, and she uttered an exclamation.

"What is the matter?" said Mrs. Gaunt, turning her head sharply round.

"A wench's glove, as I'm a living sinner," groaned Betty.

A poor little glove lay on the table; and both women eyed it like basilisks a moment. Then Betty pounced on it and examined it with the fierce keenness of her sex in such conjunctures, searching for a name or a clue.

Owing to this rapidity, Mrs. Gaunt, who stood at some distance, had not time to observe the button on the glove, or she would have recognized her own property.

"He have had a hussy with him unbeknown," said Betty, "and she have left her glove. 'Tis easy to get in by the window and out again. Only let me catch her. I'll tear her eyes out, and give him my mind. I'll have no young hussies creeping in an' out where I be."

Thus spoke the simple woman, venting her coarse domestic jealousy.

The gentlewoman said nothing, but a strange feeling traversed her heart for the first time in her life.

It was a little chill, it was a little ache, it was a little sense of sickness; none of these violent, yet all distinct. And all about what? After this curious, novel spasm at the heart, she began to be ashamed of herself for having had such a feeling.

Betty held her out the glove: and then she recognized it, and turned as red as fire.

"You know whose 'tis?" said Betty, keenly.

Mrs. Gaunt was on her guard in a moment. "Why, Betty," said she, "for shame! 'tis some penitent hath left her glove after confession. Would you belie a good man for that? Oh, lie!"

"Humph!" said Betty, doubtfully. "Then why keep it under cover? Now you can read, dame; let us see if there isn't a letter or so writ by the hand as owns this very glove."

Mrs. Gaunt declined, with cold dignity, to pry into Brother Leonard's manuscripts.

Her eye, however, darted sidelong at them, and told another tale; and, if she had been there alone, perhaps the daughter of Eve would have predominated.

Betty, inflamed by the glove, rummaged the papers in search of female handwriting. She could tell that from a man's, though she could not read either.

But there is a handwriting that the most ignorant can read at sight; and so Betty's researches were not in vain: hidden under several sheets of paper, she found a picture. She gave but one glance at it, and screamed out—"There, didn't I tell you? Here she is! the brazen, red-haired—Lawk a daisy! why, 'tis yourself."

CHAPTER III

"Me!" cried Mrs. Gaunt, in amazement: then she ran to the picture, and at sight of it every other sentiment gave way for a moment to gratified vanity. "Nay," said she, beaming and blushing, "I was never half so beautiful. What heavenly eyes!"

"The fellows to 'em be in your own head, dame, this moment."

"Seeing is believing," said Mrs. Gaunt, gaily, and in a moment she was at the priest's mirror, and inspected her eyes minutely, cocking her head this way and that. She ended by shaking it, and saying, "Nay. He has flattered them prodigiously."

"Not a jot," said Betty. "If you could see yourself in chapel, you do turn 'em up just so, and the white shows all round." Then she tapped the picture with her finger: "Oh them eyes! they were never made for the good of his soul; poor simple man."

Betty said this with sudden gravity: and now Mrs. Gaunt began to feel very awkward. "Mr. Gaunt would give fifty pounds for this," said she, to gain time: and, while she uttered that sentence, she whipped on her armour.

"I'll tell you what I think," said she, calmly: "he wished to paint a Madonna; and he must take some woman's face to aid his fancy. All the painters are driven to that. So he just took the best that came to hand, and that is not saying much, for this is a rare ill-favoured parish: and he has made an angel of her, a very angel. There, hide Me away again, or I shall long for Me—to show to my husband. I must be going; I wouldn't be caught here now for a pension."

"Well, if ye must," said Betty; "but when will ye come again?" (She hadn't got the petticoat yet.)

"Humph!" said Mrs. Gaunt, "I have done all I can for him; and perhaps more than I ought. But there's nothing to hinder you from coming to me. I'll be as good as my word; and I have an old Paduasoy, besides; you can do something with it perhaps."

"You are very good, dame," said Betty, curtsying.

Mrs. Gaunt then hurried away, and Betty looked after her very expressively, and shook her head. She had a female instinct that mischief was brewing.

Mrs. Gaunt went home in a reverie.

At the gate she found her husband, and asked him to take a turn in the garden with her.

He complied; and she intended to tell him a portion, at least, of what had occurred. She began timidly, after this fashion——"My dear, Brother Leonard is so grateful for your flowers," and then hesitated.

"I'm sure he is very welcome," said Griffith. "Why doesn't he sup with us and be sociable, as Father Francis used? Invite him; let him know he will be welcome."

Sirs. Gaunt blushed; and objected, "He never calls on us."

"Well, well, every man to his taste," said Griffith, indifferently, and proceeded to talk to her about his farm, and a sorrel mare with a white mane and tail, that he had seen, and thought it would suit her.

She humoured him, and affected a great interest in all this, and had not the courage to force the other topic on.

Next Sunday morning, after a very silent breakfast, she burst out, almost violently, "Griffith, I shall go to the parish church with you, and then we will dine together afterwards."

"You don't mean it, Kate?" said he, delighted. "Ay, but I do. Although you refused to go to chapel with me."

They went to church together, and Mrs. Gaunt's appearance there created no small sensation. She was conscious of that, but hid it, and conducted herself admirably. Her mind seemed entirely given to the service, and to a dull sermon that followed.

But at dinner she broke out, "Well, give me your church for a sleeping draught. You all slumbered, more or less: those that survived the drowsy, droning prayers, sank under the dry, dull dreary discourse. You snored, for one."

"Nay, I hope not, my dear."

"You did, then, as loud as your bass fiddle."

"And you sat there and let me!" said Griffith, reproachfully.

"To be sure I did. I was too good a wife, and too good a Christian, to wake you. Sleep is good for the body, and twaddle is not good for the soul.

I'd have slept too, if I could; but, with me going to chapel, I'm not used to sleep at that time o' day. You can't sleep, and Brother Leonard speaking."

In the afternoon came Mrs. Gough, all in her best. Mrs. Gaunt had her into her bedroom, and gave her the promised petticoat, and the old Peau de soie gown; and then, as ladies will, when their hand is once in, added first one thing, then another, till there was quite a large bundle.

"But how is it you are here so soon?" asked Mrs. Gaunt.

"Oh, we had next to no sermon to-day. He couldn't make no hand of it: dawdled on a bit; then gave us his blessing, and bundled us out."

"Then I've lost nothing," said Mrs. Gaunt.

"Not you. Well, I don't know. Mayhap if you had been there he'd have preached his best. But la, we weren't worth it."

At this conjecture Mrs. Gaunt's face burned; but she said nothing: only she cut the interview short, and dismissed Betty with her bundle.

As Betty crossed the landing, Mrs. Gaunt's new lady's-maid, Caroline Ryder, stepped accidentally, on purpose, out of an adjoining room, in which she had been lurking, and lifted her black brows in affected surprise. "What, are you going to strip the house, my woman?" said she, quietly.

Betty put down the bundle, and set her arms akimbo. "There is none on't stolen, any way," said she.

Caroline's black eyes flashed fire at this, and her cheek lost colour; but she parried the innuendo skilfully.

"Taking my perquisites on the sly, that is not so very far from stealing."

"Oh, there's plenty left for you, my fine lady. Besides, you don't want her; you can set your cap at the master, they say. I'm too old for that, and too honest into the bargain."

"Too ill-favoured, you mean, ye old harridan," said Ryder, contemptuously.

But, for reasons hereafter to be dealt with. Betty's thrust went home: and the pair were mortal enemies from that hour.

Mrs. Gaunt came down from her room discomposed: from that she became restless and irritable; so much so, indeed, that, at last, Sir. Gaunt told her, good-humouredly enough, if going to church made her ill (meaning peevish), she had better go to chapel. "You are right," said she, "and so I will."

The next Sunday she was at her post in good time.

The preacher cast an anxious glance around to see if she was there. Her quick eye saw that glance, and it gave her a demure pleasure.

This day he was more eloquent than ever: and he delivered a beautiful passage concerning those who do good in secret. In uttering these eloquent sentences, his cheek glowed, and he could not deny himself the pleasure of looking down at the lovely face that was turned up to him. Probably his look was more expressive than he intended: the celestial eyes sank under it, and were abashed, and the fair cheek burned: and then so did Leonard's at that.

Thus, subtly yet effectually, did these two minds communicate in a crowd, that never noticed nor suspected the delicate interchange of sentiment that was going on under their very eyes.

In a general way compliments did not seduce Mrs. Gaunt: she was well used to them, for one thing. Put to be praised in that sacred edifice, 'and from the pulpit, and by such an orator as Leonard, and to be praised in words so sacred and beautiful, that the ears around her drank them with delight, all this made her heart beat, and filled her with soft and sweet complacency.

And then to be thanked in public, yet, as it were, clandestinely, this gratified the furtive tendency of women.

There was no irritability this afternoon; but a gentle radiance that diffused itself on all around, and made the whole household happy; especially Griffith, whose pipe she filled, for once, with her own white hand, and talked dogs, horses, calves, hinds, cows, politics, markets, hay, to please him: and seemed interested in them all.

But the next day she changed: ill at ease, and out of spirits, and could settle to nothing.

It was very hot for one thing: and, altogether, a sort of lassitude and distaste for everything overpowered her, and she retired into the grove, and sat languidly on a seat with half-closed eyes.

But her meditations were no longer so calm and speculative as heretofore. She found her mind constantly recurring to one person, and, above all, to the discovery she had made of her portrait in his possession. She had turned it off to Betty Gough; but here, in her calm solitude and umbrageous twilight, her mind crept out of its cave, like wild and timid things at dusk, and whispered to her heart that Leonard perhaps admired her more than was safe or prudent.

Then this alarmed her, yet caused her a secret complacency: and that, her furtive satisfaction, alarmed her still more.

Now, while she sat thus absorbed, she heard a gentle footstep coming near. She looked up, and there was Leonard close to her; standing meekly with his arms crossed upon his bosom.

His being there so pat upon her thoughts, scared her out of her habitual self-command. She started up, with a faint cry, and stood panting, as if about to fly, with, her beautiful eyes turned large upon him.

He put forth a deprecating hand, and soothed her. "Forgive me, madam," said he; "I have unawares intruded on your privacy; I will retire."

"Nay," said she, falteringly, "you are welcome. But no one comes here; so I was startled;" then, recovering herself, "excuse my ill-manners. 'Tis so strange you should come to me here, of all places."

"Nay, my daughter," said the priest, "not so very strange: contemplative minds love such places. Calling one day to see you, I found this sweet and solemn grove; the like I never saw in England: and to-day I returned in hopes to profit by it. Do but look around at these tall columns; how calm, how reverend! 'Tis God's own temple not built with hands."

"Indeed it is," said Mrs. Gaunt, earnestly. Then, like a woman as she was, "So you came to see my trees, not me."

Leonard blushed. "I did not design to return without paying my respects to her who owns this temple, and is worthy of it; nay, I beg you not to think me ungrateful."

His humility, and gentle but earnest voice, made Mrs. Gaunt ashamed of her petulance. She smiled sweetly, and looked pleased. However, ere long, she attacked him again. "Father Francis used to visit us often," said she. "He made friends with my husband, too. And I never lacked an adviser while he was here."

Leonard looked so confused at this second reproach that Mrs. Gaunt regretted having uttered it. Then he said humbly that Francis was a secular priest, whereas he was convent-bred. He added, that by his years and experience Francis was better fitted to advise persons of her age and sex, in matters secular, than he was. He concluded timidly that he was ready, nevertheless, to try and advise her; but could not, in such matters, assume the authority that belongs to age and knowledge of the world.

"Nay, nay," said she, earnestly, "guide and direct my soul, and I am content."

He said, yes! that was his duty and his right.

Then, after a certain hesitation, which at once let her know what was coming, he began to thank her, with infinite grace and sweetness, for her kindness to him.

She looked him full in the face, and said she was not aware of any kindness she had shown him worth speaking of.

"That but shows," said he, "how natural it is to you to do acts of goodness. My poor room is a very bower now, and I am happy in it. I used to feel very sad there at times; but your hand has cured me."

Mrs. Gaunt coloured beautifully. "You make me ashamed," said she. "Things are come to a pass indeed if a lady may not send a few flowers and things to her spiritual father without being—thanked for it. And, oh, sir, what are earthly flowers compared with those blossoms of the soul you have shed so liberally over us? Our immortal parts were all asleep when you came here, and wakened them by the fire of your words. Eloquence! 'twas a thing I had read of, but never heard, nor thought to hear. Methought the orators and poets of the Church were all in their graves this thousand years, and she must go all the way to heaven, that would hear the soul's true music. But I know better now."

Leonard coloured high with pleasure. "Such praise from you is too sweet," he muttered. "I must not court it. The heart is full of vanity." And he deprecated further eulogy, by a movement of the hand extremely refined and, in fact, rather feminine.

Deferring to his wish, Mrs. Gaunt glided to other matters, and was naturally led to speak of the prospects of their Church, and the possibility of reconverting these islands. This had been the dream of her young heart; but marriage and maternity, and the universal coldness with which the subject had been received, had chilled her so, that of late years she had almost ceased to speak of it. Even Leonard, on a former occasion, had listened coldly to her; but now his heart was open to her. He was, in fact, quite as enthusiastic on this point as ever she had been; and then he had digested his aspirations into clearer forms. Not only had he resolved that Great Britain must be reconverted, but had planned the way to do it. His cheek glowed, his eyes gleamed, and he poured out his hopes and his plans before her with an eloquence that few mortals could have resisted.

As for this, his hearer, she was quite carried away by it. She joined herself to his plans on the spot; she begged, with tears in her eyes, to be permitted to support him in this great cause. She devoted to it her substance, her influence, and every gift that God had given her: the hours passed like minutes in this high converse; and, when the tinkling of the little bell at a distance summoned him to vespers, he left her with a gentle regret he scarcely tried to conceal, and she went slowly in like one in a dream, and the world seemed dead to her for ever.

Nevertheless, when Mrs. Ryder, combing out her long hair, gave one inadvertent tug, the fair enthusiast came back to earth, and asked her, rather sharply, who her head was running on.

Ryder, a very handsome young woman, with fine black eyes, made no reply, but only drew her breath audibly hard.

I do not very much wonder at that, nor at my having to answer that question for Mrs. Ryder. For her head was at that moment running, like any other woman's, on the man she was in love with.

And the man she was in love with was the husband of the lady, whose hair she was combing, and who put her that curious question—plump.

CHAPTER IV

This Caroline Ryder was a character almost impossible to present so as to enable the reader to recognize her should she cross his path: so great was the contradiction between what she was, and what she seemed; and so perfect was the imitation.

She looked a respectable young spinster, with a grace of manner beyond her station, and a decency and propriety of demeanour that inspired respect.

She was a married woman, separated from her husband by mutual consent: and she had had many lovers, each of whom she had loved ardently—for a little while. She was a woman that brought to bear upon foolish, culpable, loves, a mental power that would have adorned the wool-sack.

The moment prudence or waning inclination made it advisable to break with the reigning favourite, she set to work to cool him down by deliberate coldness, sullenness, insolence; and generally succeeded. But, if he was incurable, she never hesitated as to her course; she smiled again on him and looked out for another place: being an invaluable servant, she got one directly; and was off to fresh pastures.

A female rake; but with the air of a very prude.

Still the decency and propriety of her demeanour were not all hypocrisy, but half hypocrisy, and half inborn and instinctive good taste and good sense.

As dangerous a creature to herself and others as ever tied on a bonnet.

On her arrival at Hernshaw Castle she cast her eyes round to see what there was to fall in love with; and observed the gamekeeper, Tom Leicester. She gave him a smile or two that won his heart; but there she stopped: for soon the ruddy cheek, brown eyes, manly proportions, and square shoulders of her master attracted this connoisseur in masculine beauty. And then his manner was so genial and hearty, with a smile for everybody. Mrs. Ryder eyed him demurely day by day, and often opened a window slily to watch him unseen.

From that she got to throwing herself in his way: and this with such art that he never discovered it, though he fell in with her about the house six times as often as he met his wife or any other inmate.

She had already studied his character, and, whether she arranged to meet him full, or to cross him, it was always with a curtsy and a sunshiny smile; he smiled on her in his turn, and felt a certain pleasure at sight of her: for he loved to see people bright and cheerful about him.

Then she did, of her own accord, what no other master on earth would have persuaded her to do: looked over his linen; sewed on buttons for him; and sometimes the artful jade deliberately cut a button off a clean shirt, and then came to him and sewed it on during wear. This brought about a contact none knew better than she how to manage to a man's undoing. The eyelashes lowered over her work, deprecating, yet inviting,—the twenty stitches, when six would have done,—the one coy glance at leaving. All this soft witchcraft beset Griffith Gaunt, and told on him; but not as yet in the way his inamorata intended. "Kate," said he one day, "that girl of yours is worth her weight in gold."

"Indeed!" said 'Mrs. Gaunt, frigidly; "I have not discovered it."

When Caroline found that her master was single-hearted, and loved his wife too well to look elsewhere, instead of hating him, she began to love him more seriously, and to hate his wife, that haughty beauty who took such a husband as a matter of course, and held him tight without troubling her head.

It was a coarse age, and in that very county more than one wife had suffered jealous agony from her own domestic. But here the parts were inverted: the lady was at her ease; the servant paid a bitter penalty for her folly. She was now passionately in love, and had to do menial offices for her rival every hour of the day: she must sit with Mrs. Gaunt, and make her dresses, and consult with her how to set off her hateful beauty to the best advantage. She had to dress her, and look daggers at her satin skin and royal neck, and to sit behind her an hour at a time combing and brushing her long golden hair.

How she longed to tear a handful of it out, and then run away! Instead of that, her happy rival expected her to be as tender and coaxing with it as Madame de Maintenon was with the Queen's of France.

Ryder called it "yellow stuff" down in the kitchen; that was one comfort: but a feeble one; the sun came in at the lady's window, and Ryder's shapely hand was overflowed, and her eyes offended, by waves of burnished gold: and one day Griffith came in and kissed it in her very hand. His lips felt nothing but his wife's glorious hair; but, by that exquisite sensibility which the heart can convey in a moment to the very fingernails, Caroline's hand, beneath, felt the soft touch through her mistress's hair; and the enamoured hypocrite thrilled, and then sickened at her own folly.

For in her good sense could be overpowered, but never long blinded.

On the day in question she was thinking of Griffith, as usual, and wondering whether he would always prefer yellow hair to black. This actually put her off her guard for once, and she gave the rival hair a little contemptuous tug: and the reader knows what followed.

Staggered by her mistress's question, Caroline made no reply, but only panted a little, and proceeded more carefully.

But, oh the struggle it cost her not to slap both Mrs. Gaunt's fair cheeks with the backs of the brushes! And what with this struggle, and the reprimand, and the past agitations, by-and-by the comb ceased, and the silence was broken by faint sobs.

Mrs. Gaunt turned calmly round and looked full at her hysterical handmaid.

"What is to do?" said she. "Is it because I chid you, child? Nay, you need not take that to heart; it is just my way: I can bear anything but my hair pulled." With this she rose and poured some drops of sal-volatile into water, and put it to her secret rival's lips: it was kindly done, but with that sort of half contemptuous and thoroughly cold pity women are apt to show to women, and especially when one of them is Mistress and the other is Servant.

Still it cooled the extreme hatred Caroline had nursed, and gave her a little twinge, and awakened her intelligence. Now her intelligence was truly remarkable when not blinded by passion. She was a woman with one or two other masculine traits beside her roving heart. For instance, she could sit and think hard and practically for hours together: and on these occasions her thoughts were never dreamy and vague; it was no brown study, but good hard thinking. She would knit her coal-black brows, like Lord Thurlow himself, and realize the situation, and weigh the pros and cons with a steady judicial power rarely found in her sex: and, nota bene, when once her mind had gone through this process, then she would act with almost monstrous resolution.

She now shut herself up in her own room for some hours and weighed the matter carefully.

The conclusion she arrived at was this: that, if she stayed at Hernshaw Castle, there would be mischief; and probably she herself would be the principal sufferer to the end of the chapter, as she was now.

She said to herself, "I shall go mad, or else expose myself, and be turned away with loss of character; and then what will become of me, and my child? Better lose life or reason than character. I know what I have to go through; I have left a man ere now with my heart tugging at me to stay beside him. It is a terrible wrench: and then all seems dead for a long while without him. But the world goes on and takes you round with it; and by-and-by you find there are as good fish left in the sea as ever came out on't. I'll go, while I've sense enough left to see I must."

The very next day she came to Mrs. Gaunt and said she wished to leave. "Certainly," said Mrs. Gaunt, coldly. "May I ask the reason?"

"Oh, I have no complaint to make, ma'am, none whatever; but I am not happy here; and I wish to go when my month's up, or sooner, ma'am, if you could suit yourself."

Mrs. Gaunt considered a moment: then she said, "You came all the way from Gloucestershire to me: had you not better give the place a fair trial? I have had two or three good servants that felt uncomfortable at first; but they soon found out my ways, and stayed with me till they married. As for leaving me before your month, that is out of the question." To this Ryder said not a word, but merely vented a little sigh, half dogged, half submissive; and went cat-like about, arranging her mistress's things with admirable precision and neatness. Mrs. Gaunt watched her, without seeming to do so, and observed that her discontent did not in the least affect her punctual discharge of her duties. Said Mrs. Gaunt to herself, "This servant is a treasure: she shall not go." And Ryder to herself, "Well, 'tis but for a month; and then no power shall keep me here."

CHAPTER V

Not long after these events came the county ball. Griffith was there, but no Mrs. Gaunt. This excited surprise, and, among the gentlemen, disappointment. They asked Griffith if she was unwell; he thanked them drily, she was very well; and that was all they could get out of him. But to the ladies he let out that she had given up balls, and, indeed, all reasonable pleasures. "She does nothing but fast, and pray, and visit the sick." He added, with rather a weak smile: "I see next to nothing of her." A minx stood by and put in her word. "You should catch the small-pox; then who knows? she might look in upon *you*."

Griffith laughed, but not heartily. In truth, Mrs. Gaunt's religious fervour knew no bounds. Absorbed in pious schemes and religious duties, she had little time, and much distaste, for frivolous society; invited none but the devout, and found polite excuses for not dining abroad. She sent her husband into the world alone, and laden with apologies. "My wife is turned saint. 'Tis a sin to dance, a sin to hunt, a sin to enjoy ourselves. We are here to fast and pray, and build schools, and go to church twice a day."

And so he went about publishing his household ill; but, to tell the truth, a secret satisfaction peeped through his lugubrious accents. An ugly saint is an unmixed calamity to jolly fellows; but to be lord and master, and possessor of a beautiful saint, was not without its piquant charm. His jealousy was dormant, not extinct; and Kate's piety tickled that foible, not wounded it. He found himself the rival of heaven; and the successful rival; for, let her be ever so strict, ever so devout, she must give her husband many comforts she could not give to heaven.

This soft and piquant phase of the passion did not last long. All things are progressive.

Brother Leonard was director now as well as confessor; his visits became frequent; and Mrs. Gaunt often quoted his authority for her acts or her sentiments. So Griffith began to suspect that the change in his wife was entirely due to Leonard; and that with all her eloquence and fervour she was but a priest's echo. This galled him. To be sure Leonard was only an ecclesiastic; but, if he had been a woman, Griffith was the man to wince. His wife to lean so on another: his wife to withdraw from the social pleasures she had hitherto shared with him; and all because another human creature disapproved them. He writhed in silence a while, and then remonstrated. He was met at first with ridicule: "Are you going to be jealous of my confessor?" and, on repeating the offence, with a kind, but grave admonition, that silenced him for the time, but did not cure him, nor even convince him.

The facts were too strong: Kate was no longer to him the genial companion she had been; gone was the ready sympathy with which she had listened to all his little earthly concerns; and, as for his hay-making, he might as well talk about it to an iceberg as to the partner of his bosom.

He was genial by nature, and could not live without sympathy. He sought it in the parlour of the "Red Lion."

Mrs. Gaunt's high-bred nostrils told her where he haunted, and it caused her dismay. Woman-like, instead of opening her battery at once, she wore a gloomy and displeased air, which a few months ago would have served her turn and brought about an explanation at once; but Griffith took it for a stronger dose of religious sentiment, and trundled off to the "Red Lion," all the more.

So then at last she spoke her mind; and asked him how he could lower himself so, and afflict her.

"Oh!" said he, doggedly, "this house is too cold for me now. My mate is priest-rid. Plague on the knave that hath put coldness 'twixt thee and me."

Mrs. Gaunt froze visibly, and said no more at that time.

One bit of sunshine remained in the house and shone brighter than ever on its chilled master; shone through two black, seducing eyes.

Some three months before the date we have now reached, Caroline Ryder's two boxes were packed and corded ready to go next day. She had quietly persisted in her resolution to leave, and Mrs. Gaunt, though secretly angry, had been just and magnanimous enough to give her a good character.

Now female domestics are like the little birds; if that great hawk, their mistress, follows them about, it is a deadly grievance; but if she does not, they follow her about, and pester her with idle questions, and invite the beak and claws of petty tyranny and needless interference.

So the afternoon before she was to leave, Caroline Ryder came to her mistress's room on some imaginary business. She was not there. Ryder, forgetting that it did not matter a straw, proceeded to hunt her everywhere; and at last ran out with only her cap on to "the Dame's Haunt," and there she was; but not alone: she was walking up and down with Brother Leonard. Their backs were turned, and Ryder came up behind them. Leonard was pacing gravely, with his head gently drooping as usual. Mrs. Gaunt was walking elastically, and discoursing with great fire and animation.

Ryder glided after, noiseless as a serpent, more bent on wondering and watching now than on overtaking; for inside the house her mistress showed none of this charming vivacity.

Presently the keen black eyes observed a "trifle light as air" that made them shine again.

She turned and wound herself amongst the trees, and disappeared. Soon after she was in her own room, a changed woman. With glowing cheeks, sparkling eyes, and nimble fingers, she uncorded her boxes, unpacked her things, and placed them neatly in the drawers.

What more had she seen than I have indicated?

Only this: Mrs. Gaunt, in the warmth of discourse, laid her hand lightly for a moment on the priest's elbow: that was nothing, she had laid the same hand on Ryder; for, in fact, it was a little womanly way she had, and a hand that settled like down. But this time, as she withdrew it again, that delicate hand seemed to speak; it did not leave Leonard's elbow all at once, it glided slowly away, first the palm, then the fingers, and so parted lingeringly.

The other woman saw this subtle touch of womanhood, coupled it with Mrs. Gaunt's vivacity and the air of happiness that seemed to inspire her whole eloquent person, and formed a harsh judgment on the spot, though she could not see the lady's face.

When Mrs. Gaunt came in she met her, and addressed her thus: "If you please, ma'am, have you any one coming in my place?"

Mrs. Gaunt looked her full in the face. "You know I have not," said she, haughtily.

"Then, if it is agreeable to you, ma'am, I will stay. To be sure the place is dull; but I have got a good mistress-and— —"

"That will do, Ryder: a servant has always her own reasons, and never tells them to her mistress. You can stay this time; but the next, you go; and once for all. I am not to be trifled with."

Ryder called up a look all submission, and retired with an obeisance. But, once out of sight, she threw off the mask and expanded with insolent triumph. "Yes, I have my own reasons," said she. "Keep you the priest, and I'll take the man."

From that hour Caroline Ryder watched her mistress like a lynx, and hovered about her master, and poisoned him slowly with vague insidious hints.

CHAPTER VI

Brother Leonard, like many holy men, was vain. Not but what he had his gusts of humility and diffidence; only they blew over.

At first, as you may perhaps remember, he doubted his ability to replace Father Francis as Mrs. Gaunt's director; but after a slight disclaimer, he did replace him, and had no more misgivings as to his fitness. But his tolerance and good sense were by no means equal to his devotion and his persuasive powers; and so his advice in matters spiritual and secular somehow sowed the first seeds of conjugal coolness in Hernshaw Castle.

And now Ryder slily insinuated into Griffith's ear that the mistress told the priest everything, and did nothing but by his advice. Thus the fire already kindled was fanned by an artful woman's breath.

Griffith began to hate Brother Leonard, and to show it so plainly and rudely that Leonard shrank from the encounter, and came less often, and stayed but a few minutes. Then Mrs. Gaunt remonstrated gently with Griffith, but received short sullen replies. Then, as the servile element of her sex was comparatively small in her, she turned bitter and cold, and avenged Leonard indirectly, but openly, with those terrible pins and needles a beloved woman has ever at command.

Then Griffith became moody, and downright unhappy, and went more and more to the "Red Lion," seeking comfort there now as well as company.

Mrs. Gaunt saw, and had fits of irritation, and fits of pity, and sore perplexity. She knew she had a good husband; and, instead of taking him to heaven with her, she found that each step she made with Leonard's help towards the angelic life, seemed somehow to be bad for Griffith's soul, and for his earthly happiness.

She blamed herself; she blamed Griffith; she blamed the Protestant heresy; she blamed everybody and everything—except Brother Leonard.

One Sunday afternoon Griffith sat on his own lawn, silently smoking his pipe. Mrs. Gaunt came to him, and saw an air of dejection on his genial face. Her heart yearned. She sat down beside him on the bench, and sighed; then he sighed too.

"My dear," said she, sweetly, "fetch out your viol da gambo, and we will sing a hymn or two together here this fine afternoon. We can praise God together, though we must pray apart; alas that it is so."

"With all my heart," said Griffith. "Nay, I forgot; my viol da gambo is not here. 'Tis at the 'Red Lion.'"

"At the 'Red Lion!'" said she, bitterly. "What, do you sing there as well as drink? Oh, husband, how can you so bemean yourself?"

"What is a poor man to do, whose wife is priest-ridden, and got to be no company—except for angels?"

"I did not come here to quarrel," said she, coldly and sadly. Then they were both silent a minute. Then she got up and left him.

Brother Leonard, like many earnest men, was rather intolerant. He urged on Mrs. Gaunt that she had too many Protestants in her household: her cook and her nursemaid ought, at all events, to be Catholics. Mrs. Gaunt on this was quite ready to turn them both off, and that without disguise. But Leonard dissuaded her from so violent a measure. She had better take occasion to part with one of them, and by-and-by with the other.

The nursemaid was the first to go, and her place was filled by a Roman Catholic. Then the cook received warning. But this did not pass off so quietly: Jane Bannister was a buxom hearty woman, well liked by her fellow-servants; her parents lived in the village, and she had been six years with the Gaunts, and her honest heart clung to them. She took to crying; used to burst out in the middle of her work, or while conversing with fitful cheerfulness on ordinary topics.

One day Griffith found her crying, and Ryder consoling her as carelessly and contemptuously as possible.

"Hey-day, lasses," said he; "what is your trouble?"

At this Jane's tears flowed in a stream, and Ryder made no reply, but waited.

At last, and not till the third or fourth time of asking, Jane blurted out that she had got the sack; such was her homely expression, dignified, however, by honest tears.

"What for?" asked Griffith, kindly.

"Nay, sir," sobbed Jane, "that is what I want to know. Our Dame ne'er found a fault in me; and now she does pack me off like a dog. Me that have been here this six years, and got to feel at home. What will father say? He'll give me a hiding. For two pins I'd drown myself in the mere."

"Come, you must not blame the mistress," said the sly Ryder. "She is a good mistress as ever breathed: 'tis all the priest's doings. I'll tell you the truth, master, if you will pass me your word I shan't be sent away for it."

"I pledge you my word as a gentleman," said Griffith.

"Well, then, sir, Jane's fault is yours and mine. She is not a papist; and that is why she is to go. How I come to know, I listened in the next room, and heard the priest tell our dame she must send away two of us, and have Catholics. The priest's word it is law in this house; 'twas in March he gave the order: Harriet, she went in May, and now poor Jane is to go—for walking to church behind you, sir. But there, Jane, I believe he would get our very master out of the house if he could; and then what would become of us all?"

Griffith turned black, and then ashy pale, under this venomous tongue, and went away without a word, looking dangerous.

Ryder looked after him, and her black eye glittered with a kind of fiendish beauty.

Jane, having told her mind, now began to pluck up a little spirit. "Mrs. Ryder," said she, "I never thought to like you so well;" and, with that, gave her a great, hearty, smacking kiss; which Ryder, to judge by her countenance, relished, as epicures albumen. "I won't cry no more. After all, this house is no place for us that be women: 'tis a fine roost to be sure! where the hen she crows and the cock do but cluck."

Town-bred Ryder laughed at the rustic maid's simile; and, not to be out-done in metaphor, told her there were dogs that barked, and dogs that bit. "Our master is one of those that bite. I've done the priest's business. He is as like to get the sack as you are."

Griffith found his wife seated on the lawn reading. He gulped down his ire as well as he could; but nevertheless his voice trembled a little with suppressed passion.

"So Jane is turned off now," said he.

"I don't know about being turned off," replied Mrs. Gaunt, calmly; "but she leaves me next month, and Cicely Davis comes back."

"And Cicely Davis is a useless slut that cannot boil a potato fit to eat; but then she is a Papist, and poor Jenny is a Protestant, and can cook a dinner."

"My dear," said Mrs. Gaunt, "do not you trouble about the servants; leave them to me."

"And welcome; but this is not your doing, it is that Leonard's: and I cannot allow a Popish priest to turn off all my servants that are worth their salt. Come, Kate, you used to be a sensible woman, and a tender wife: now I ask you, is a young bachelor a fit person to govern a man's family?"

Mrs. Gaunt laughed in his face. "A young bachelor!" said she; "whoever heard of such a term applied to a priest: and a saint upon earth?"

"Why, he is not married, so he must be a bachelor; and I say again it is monstrous for a young bachelor to come between old married folk, and hear all their secrets, and have a finger in every pie, and set up to be master of my house, and order my wife to turn away my servants for going to church behind me. Why not turn me away too? Their fault is mine."

"Griffith, you are in a passion, and I begin to think you want to put me in one."

"Well, perhaps I am. Job's patience went at last, and mine has been sore tried this many a month. 'Twas bad enough when the man was only your confessor: you told him everything, and you don't tell me everything. He knew your very heart, better than I do, and that was a bitter thing for me to bear that love you and have no secrets from you. But every man who marries a Catholic must endure this; so I put a good face on it, though my heart was often sore; 'twas the price I had to pay for my pearl of womankind. But since he set up your governor as well, you are a changed woman; you shun company abroad, you freeze my friends at home. You have made the house so cold that I am fain to seek the 'Red Lion' for a smile or a kindly word: and now, to please this fanatical priest, you would turn away the best servants I have, and put useless, dirty slatterns in their place, that happen to be Papists. You did not use to be so uncharitable, nor so unreasonable. 'Tis the priest's doing. He is my secret, underhand enemy; I feel him undermining me, inch by inch, and I can bear it no longer. I must make a stand somewhere, and I may as well make it here; for Jenny is a good girl, and her folk live in the village, and she helps them. Think better of it, Kate, and let the poor wench stay, though she does go to church behind your husband."

"Griffith," said Mrs. Gaunt, "I might retort, and say that you are a changed man; for to be sure you did never use to interfere between me and my maids. Are you sure some mischief-making woman is not advising you? But there, do not let us chafe one another, for you know we are hot-tempered both of us. Well, leave it for the present, my dear; prithee let me think it over till to-morrow, at all events, and try if I can satisfy you."

The jealous husband saw through this proposal directly. He turned purple. "That is to say, you must ask your priest first for leave to show your husband one grain of respect and affection, and not make him quite a cipher in his own house. No, Kate, no man who respects himself will let another man come between himself and the wife of his bosom. This business is between you and me; I will brook no interference in it; and I tell you plainly, if you turn this poor lass off to please this d——d priest, I'll turn the priest off to please her and her folk. They are as good as he is, any way."

The bitter contempt with which he spoke of Brother Leonard, and this astounding threat, imported a new and dangerous element into the discussion: it stung Mrs. Gaunt beyond bearing. She turned with flashing eyes upon Griffith.

"As good as he is? The scum of my kitchen! You will make me hate the mischief-making hussy. She shall pack out of the house to-morrow morning."'

"Then I say that priest shall never darken my doors again."

"Then I say they are my doors, not yours; and that holy man shall brighten them whenever he will."

If to strike an adversary dumb is the tongue's triumph, Mrs. Gaunt was victorious: for Griffith gasped, but did not reply.

They faced each other, pale with fury; but no more words.

No: an ominous silence succeeded this lamentable answer, like the silence that follows a thunder-clap.

Griffith stood still awhile, benumbed as it were, by the cruel stroke; then cast one speaking look of anguish and reproach upon her, drew himself haughtily up, and stalked away like a wounded lion.

Well said the ancients that anger is a short madness. When we reflect in cold blood on the things we have said in hot, how impossible they seem! how out of character with our real selves! And this is one of the recognized symptoms of mania.

There were few persons could compare with Mrs. Gaunt in native magnanimity; yet how ungenerous a stab had she given.

And had he gone on, she would have gone on; but when he turned silent at her bitter thrust, and stalked away from her, she came to herself almost directly.

She thought, "Good God! what have I said to him?"

And the flush of shame came to her cheek, and her eyes filled with tears.

He saw them not; he had gone away, wounded to the heart.

You see it was true. The house was hers; tied up as tight as wax. The very money (his own money) that had been spent on the place, had become hers by being expended on real property; he could not reclaim it; he was her lodger; a dependant on her bounty.

During all the years they had lived together she had never once assumed the proprietor. On the contrary, she put him forward as the Squire, and slipped quietly into the background. Bene latuit. But, lo! let a hand be put out to offend her saintly favourite, and that moment she could waken her husband from his dream, and put him down into his true legal position with a word. The matrimonial throne for him till he resisted her priest; and then, a stool at her feet, and his.

He was enraged as well as hurt; but being a true lover, his fury was levelled not at the woman who had hurt him, but at the man who stood out of sight and set her on.

By this time the reader knows his good qualities, and his defects; superior to his wife in one or two things, he was by no means so thorough a gentleman as she was a lady. He had begun to make a party with his own servants against the common enemy; and, in his wrath, he now took another step, or rather a stride, in the same direction. As he hurried away to the public-house, white with ire, he met his gamekeeper coming in with a bucketful of fish fresh caught. "What have ye got there?" said Griffith, roughly; not that he was angry with the man, but that his very skin was full of wrath, and it must exude. Mr. Leicester did not relish the tone, and replied, bluntly and sulkily, "Pike for our Papists." The answer, though rude, did not altogether displease Griffith; it smacked of odium theologicum, a sentiment he was learning to understand. "Put 'em down, and listen to me, Thomas Leicester," said he. And his manner was now so impressive that Leicester put down the bucket with ludicrous expedition, and gaped at him.

"How, my man, why do I keep you here?"

"To take care of your game, Squire, I do suppose."

"What? when you are the worst gamekeeper in the county. How many poachers do you catch in the year? They have only to set one of their gang to treat you at the public-house on a moonshiny night, and the rest can have all my pheasants at roost while you are boozing and singing."

"Like my betters in the parlour," muttered Tom.

"But that is not all," continued Gaunt, pretending not to hear him. "You wire my rabbits, and sell them in the town. Don't go to deny it; fore I've half a dozen to prove it." Mr. Leicester looked very uncomfortable. His master continued—"I have known it this ten months, yet you are none the worse for't. Now, why do I keep you here, that any other gentleman in my place would send to Carlisle gaol on a justice's warrant?"

Mr. Leicester, who had thought his master blind, and was so suddenly undeceived, hung his head and snivelled out, "'Tis because you have a good heart, Squire, and would not ruin a poor fellow for an odd rabbit or two."

"Stuff and nonsense!" cried Gaunt. "Speak your mind, for once, or else begone for a liar as well as a knave."

Thus appealed to, Leicester's gipsy eyes roved to and fro as if he were looking for some loophole to escape by; but at last he faced the situation.

He said, with a touch of genuine feeling, "D——n the rabbits! I wish my hand had withered ere I touched one on them." But after this preface he sunk his voice to a whisper, and said, "I see what you are driving at, Squire; and since there is nobody with us (he took off his cap)—why, sir, 'tis this here mole I am in debt to, no doubt."

Then the gentleman and his servant looked one another silently in the face, and what with their standing in the same attitude and being both excited and earnest, the truth must be owned, a certain family likeness came out. Certainly, their eyes were quite unlike. Leicester had his gipsy mother's: black, keen, and restless. Gaunt had his mother's: brown, calm, and steady. But the two men had the same stature, the same manly mould and square shoulders; and, though Leicester's cheek was brown as a berry, his forehead was singularly white for a man in his rank of life, and over his left temple, close to the roots of the hair, was an oblong mole as black as ink, that bore a close resemblance in appearance and position to his master's.

"Tom Leicester; I have been insulted."

"That won't pass, sir. Who is the man?"

"One that I cannot call out like a gentleman, and yet I must not lay on him with my cane, or I am like to get the sack, as well as my servants. 'Tis the Popish priest, lad; Brother Leonard, own brother to Old Kick; he has got our Dame's ear, she cannot say him 'nay.' She is turning away all my people, and filling the house with Papists, to please him. And when I interfered, she as good as told me I should go next; and so I shall, I or else that priest."

This little piece of exaggeration fired Tom Leicester. "Say ye so, Squire? then just you whisper a word in my ear, and George and I will lay that priest by the heels, and drag him through the horse-pond. He won't come here to trouble you after that, I know."

Gaunt's eyes flashed triumph. "A friend in need is a friend indeed," said he. "Ay, you are right, lad. There must be no broken bones, and no bloodshed; the horse-pond is the very thing: and if she discharges you for it, take no heed of her. You shall never leave Hernshaw Castle for that good deed; or, if you do, I'll go with you; for the world it is wide, and I'll never live a servant in the house where I have been a master." They then put their heads together and concerted the means by which the priest at his very next visit was to be decoyed into the neighbourhood of the horse-pond.

And then they parted, and Griffith went to the "Red Lion." And a pair of black eyes that had slily watched this singular interview from an upper window, withdrew quietly; and soon after, Tom Leicester found himself face to face with their owner, the sight of whom always made his heart beat a little faster.

Caroline Ryder had been rather cold to him of late; it was therefore a charming surprise when she met him, all wreathed in smiles, and, drawing him apart, began to treat him like a bosom friend, and tell him what had passed between the master, and her and Jane. Confidence begets confidence; and so Tom told her in turn that the Squire and the Dame had come to words over it. "However," said he, "'tis all the priest's fault; but bide awhile, all of ye."

With this mysterious hint he meant to close his revelations. But Ryder intended nothing of the kind. Her keen eye had read the looks and gestures of Gaunt and Leicester, and these had shown her that something very strange and serious was going on. She had come out expressly to learn what it was, and Tom was no match for her arts. She so smiled on him, and agreed with him, and led him, and drew him, and pumped him, that she got it all out of him on a promise of secresy. She then entered into it with spirit, and being what they called a scholar, undertook to write a paper for Tom and his helper to pin on the priest's back. No sooner said than done. She left him, and speedily returned with the following document written out in large and somewhat straggling letters:——

"HONEST FOLK, BEHOLD A
MISCHIEVIOUS PRIEST, WHICH
FOR CAUSING OF STRIFE
'TWIXT MAN AND WYFE
HATH MADE ACQUAINTAUNCE
WITH SQUIRE'S HORSE-POND."

And so a female conspirator was added to the plot.

Mrs. Gaunt co-operated too, but, need I say, unconsciously.

She was unhappy, and full of regret at what she had said. She took herself severely to task and drew a very unfavourable comparison between herself and Brother Leonard. "How ill," she thought, "am I fitted to carry out that meek saint's views. See what my ungoverned temper has done." So then, having made so great a mistake, she thought the best thing she could do was to seek advice of Leonard at once. She was not without hopes he would tell her to postpone the projected change in her household, and so soothe her offended husband directly.

She wrote a line requesting Leonard to call on her as soon as possible, and advise her in a great difficulty; and she gave this note to Ryder, and told her to send the groom off with it at once.

Ryder squeezed the letter, and peered into it, and gathered its nature before she gave it to the groom to take to Leonard.

When he was gone she went and told Tom Leicester, and he chuckled, and made his preparations accordingly.

Then she retired to her own room and went through a certain process I have indicated before as one of her habits: knitted her great black brows, and pondered the whole situation with a mental power that was worthy of a nobler sphere and higher materials.

Her practical reverie, so to speak, continued until she was rung for to dress her mistress for dinner.

Griffith was so upset, so agitated and restless, he could not stay long in any one place, not even in the "Red Lion." So he came home to dinner, though he had mighty little appetite for it. And this led to another little conjugal scene.

Mrs. Gaunt mounted the great oak staircase to dress for dinner, languidly, as ladies are apt to do, when reflection and regret come after excitement.

Presently she heard a quick foot behind her: she knew it directly for her husband's, and her heart yearned. She did not stop, nor turn her head: womanly pride withheld her from direct submission; but womanly tenderness and tact opened a way to reconciliation. She drew softly aside, almost to the wall, and went slower; and her hand, her sidelong drooping head, and her whole eloquent person, whispered plainly enough, "If somebody would like to make friends, here is the door open."

Griffith saw, but was too deeply wounded: he passed her without stopping (the staircase was eight feet broad).

But as he passed he looked at her and sighed, for he saw she was sorry.

She heard, and sighed too. Poor things, they had lived so happy together for years.

He went on.

Her pride bent: "Griffith!" said she, very timidly. He turned and stopped at that.

"Sweetheart," she murmured, "I was to blame. I was ungenerous. I forgot myself. Let me recall my words. You know they did not come from my heart."

"You need not tell me that," said Griffith doggedly. "I have no quarrel with you, and never will. You but do what you are bidden, and say what you are bidden. I take the wound from you as best I may: the man that set you on, 'tis him I'll be revenged on."

"Alas! that you will think so," said she. "Believe me, dearest, that holy man would be the first to rebuke me for rebelling against my husband and flouting him. Oh, how could I say such things? I thank you, and love you dearly for being so blind to my faults; but I must not abuse your blindness. Father Leonard will put me to penance for the fault you forgive. He will hear no excuses. Prithee, now, be more just to that good man."

Griffith listened quietly, with a cold sneer upon his lip; and this was his reply: "Till that mischief-making villain came between you and me, you never gave me a bitter word: we were the happiest pair in Cumberland. But now what are we? And what shall we be in another year or two?—REVENGE!!"

He had begun gravely enough, but suddenly burst into an ungovernable rage; and as he yelled out that furious word his face was convulsed and ugly to look at; very ugly.

Mrs. Gaunt started: she had not seen that vile expression in his face for many a year; but she knew it again.

"Ay!" he cried, "he has made me drink a bitter cup this many a day. But I'll force as bitter a one down his throat, and you shall see it done."

Mrs. Gaunt turned pale at this violent threat; but being a high-spirited woman, she stiffened and hid her apprehensions loftily. "Madman that you are," said she. "I throw away excuses on Jealousy, and I waste reason upon phrenzy. I'll say no more things to provoke you; but, to be sure, 'tis I that am offended now, and deeply too, as you will find."

"So be it," said Griffith, sullenly; then, grinding his teeth, "he shall pay for that too."

Then he went to his dressing-room, and she to her bedroom. Griffith hating Leonard, and Kate deeply indignant with Griffith.

And, ere her blood could cool, she was subjected to the keen, cold, scrutiny of another female, and that female a secret rival.

CHAPTER VII

Would you learn what men gain by admitting a member of the fair sex into their conspiracies? read the tragedy of Venice Preserved; and, by way of afterpiece, this little chapter.

Mrs. Gaunt sat pale and very silent, and Caroline Ryder stood behind, doing up her hair into a magnificent structure that added eight inches to the lady's height: and in this operation her own black hair and keen black eyes came close to the golden hair and deep blue eyes, now troubled, and made a picture striking by contrast.

As she was putting the finishing touches, she said, quietly, "If you please, Dame, I have somewhat to tell you."

Mrs. Gaunt sighed wearily, expecting some very minute communication.

"Well, Dame, I dare say I am risking my place, but I can't help it."

"Another time, Ryder," said Mrs. Gaunt. "I am in no humour to be worried with my servants' squabbles."

"Nay, madam, 'tis not that at all: 'tis about Father Leonard. Sure you would not like him to be drawn through the horse-pond; and that is what they mean to do next time he comes here."

In saying these words, the jade contrived to be adjusting Mrs. Gaunt's dress. The lady's heart gave a leap, and the servant's cunning finger felt it, and then felt a shudder run all over that stately frame. But after that Mrs. Gaunt seemed to turn to steel. She distrusted Ryder, she could not tell why; distrusted her, and was upon her guard.

"You must be mistaken," said she. "Who would dare to lay hands on a priest in my house?"

"Well, Dame, you see they egg one another on. Don't ask me to betray my fellow-servants; but let us baulk them. I don't deceive you, Dame: if the good priest shows his face here, he will be thrown into the horse-pond, and sent home with a ticket pinned to his back. Them that is to do it are on the watch now, and have got their orders; and 'tis a burning shame. To be sure I am not a Catholic; but religion is religion, and a more heavenly face I never saw: and for it to be dragged through a filthy horse-pond!"

Mrs. Gaunt clutched her inspector's arm and turned pale. "The villains! the fiends!" she gasped. "Go ask your master to come to me this moment."

Ryder took a step or two, then stopped. "Alack, Dame," said she, "that is not the way to do. You may be sure the others would not dare, if my master had not shown them his mind."

Mrs. Gaunt stopped her ears. "Don't tell me that he has ordered this impious, cruel, cowardly act. He is a lion: and this comes from the heart of cowardly curs. What is to be done, woman? tell me; for you are cooler than I am."

"Well, Dame, if I were in your place, I'd just send him a line, and bid him stay away till the storm blows over."

"You are right. But who is to carry it? My own servants are traitors to me."

"I'll carry it myself."

"You shall. Put on your hat, and run through the wood; that is the shortest way."

She wrote a few lines on a large sheet of paper, for note-paper there was none in those days; sealed it, and gave it to Ryder.

Ryder retired to put on her hat, and pry into the letter with greedy eyes.

It ran thus:— —

> "DEAR FATHER AND FRIEND,—You must come hither no more at present. Ask the bearer why this is, for I am ashamed to put it on paper. Pray for them: for you can, but I cannot. Pray for me, too, bereft for a time of your counsels. I shall come and confess to you in a few days, when we are all cooler; but you shall honour his house no more. Obey me in this one thing, who shall obey you in all things else, and am
>
> "Your indignant and sorrowful daughter,
>
> "CATHERINE GAUNT."

"No more than that?" said Ryder. "Ay, she guessed as I should look."

She whipped on her hat and went out.

Who should she meet, or, I might say, run against, at the hall door, but Father Leonard.

He had come at once in compliance with Mrs. Gaunt's request.

CHAPTER VIII

Mrs. Ryder uttered a little scream of dismay. The priest smiled, and said, sweetly, "Forgive me, mistress, I fear I startled you."

"Indeed you did, sir," said she. She looked furtively round, and saw Leicester and his underling on the watch.

Leicester, unaware of her treachery, made her a signal of intelligence.

She responded to it, to gain time.

It was a ticklish situation. Some would have lost their heads. Ryder was alarmed, but all the more able to defend her plans. Her first move, as usual with such women, was—a lie.

"Our Dame is in the Grove, sir," said she. "I am to bring you to her."

The priest bowed his head, gravely, and moved towards the Grove with downcast eyes. Ryder kept close to him for a few steps; then she ran to Leicester, and whispered, hastily, "Go you to the stable-gate: I'll bring him round that way: hide now; he suspects."

"Ay, ay," said Leicester; and the confiding pair slipped away round a corner to wait for their victim.

Ryder hurried him into the Grove, and, as soon as she had got him out of hearing, told him the truth.

He turned pale; for these delicate organizations do not generally excel in courage.

Ryder pitied him, and something of womanly feeling began to mingle with her plans. "They 'shall not lay a finger on you, sir," said she. "I'll scratch and scream, and bring the whole parish out sooner; but the best way is not to give them the chance: please you follow me." And she hurried him through the Grove, and then into an unfrequented path of the great wood.

When they were safe from pursuit she turned and looked at him. He was a good deal agitated; but the uppermost sentiment was gratitude. It soon found words, and, as usual, happy ones. He thanked her with dignity and tenderness for the service she had done him, and asked her if she was a Catholic.

"No," said she.

At that his countenance fell, but only for a moment. "Ah! would you were," he said, earnestly. So then added, sweetly, "To be sure I have all the more reason to be grateful to you."

"You are very welcome, reverend sir," said Ryder, graciously. "Religion is religion: and 'tis a barbarous thing that violence should be done to men of your cloth."

Having thus won his heart, the artful woman began at one and the same time to please and to probe him. "Sir," said she, "be of good heart; they have done you no harm, and themselves no good: my mistress will hate them for it, and love you all the more."

Father Leonard's pale cheek coloured all over at these words, though he said nothing.

"Since they won't let you come to her, she will come to you."

"Do you think so?" said he, faintly.

"Nay, I am sure of it, sir. So would any woman. We still follow our hearts, and get our way by hook or by crook."

Again the priest coloured either with pleasure or with shame, or with both; and the keen feminine eye perused him with microscopic power. She waited, to give him an opportunity of talking to her and laying bare his feelings; but he was either too delicate, too cautious, or too pure.

So then she suddenly affected to remember her mistress's letter. She produced it with an apology. He took it with unfeigned eagerness, and read it in silence; and, having read it, he stood patient, with the tears in his eyes. Ryder eyed him with much curiosity and a little pity.

"Don't you take on for that," said she. "Why, she will be more at her ease when she visits you at your place than here; and she won't give you up, I promise."

The priest trembled, and Ryder saw it.

"But, my daughter," said he, "I am perplexed and grieved. It seems that I make mischief in your house: that is an ill office; I fear it is my duty to retire from this place altogether, rather than cause dissension between those whom the Church by holy sacrament hath bound together." So saying, he hung his head and sighed.

Ryder eyed him with a little pity, but more contempt.

"Why take other people's faults on your back?" said she. "My mistress is tied to a man she does not love; but that is not your fault; and he is jealous of you that never gave him cause. If I was a man he should not accuse me—for nothing: nor set his man on to drag me through a horse-pond—for nothing. I'd have the sweet as well as the bitter."

Father Leonard turned and looked at her with a face full of terror. Some beautiful, honeyed fiend seemed to be entering his heart and tempting it.

"Oh, hush! my daughter, hush!" he said; "what words are these for a virtuous woman to speak, and a priest to hear?"

"There, I have offended you by my blunt way," said the cajoling hussy, in soft and timid tones.

"Nay, not so; but oh speak not so lightly of things that peril the immortal soul."

"Well, I have done," said Ryder. "You are out of danger now; so give you good day."

He stopped her. "What, before I have thanked you for your goodness? Ah, Mistress Ryder, 'tis on these occasions a priest sins by longing for riches to reward his benefactors. I have nought to offer you but this ring: it was my mother's, my dear mother's."

He took it off his finger to give it her.

But the little bit of goodness that cleaves even to the heart of an intriguante revolted against her avarice.

"Nay, poor soul, I'll not take it," said she; and put her hands before her eyes, not to see it, for she knew she could not look at it long and spare it.

With this she left him; but, ere she had gone far, her cunning and curiosity gained the upper hand again, and she whipped behind a great tree and crouched, invisible all but her nose and one piercing eye.

She saw the priest make a few steps homewards, then look around, then take Mrs. Gaunt's letter out of his pocket, press it passionately to his lips, and hide it tenderly in his bosom.

This done he went home with his eyes on the ground as usual, and measured steps. And to all who met him he seemed a creature in whom religion had conquered all human frailty.

Caroline Ryder hurried home with cruel exultation in her black eyes. But she soon found that the first thing she had to do was to defend herself. Leicester and his man met her, and the former looked gloomy, and the latter reproached her bitterly; called her a double-faced jade, and said he would tell the Squire of the trick she had played them. But Ryder had her story ready in a moment. "'Tis you I have saved, not him," said she. "He is something more than mortal: why, he told me of his own accord what you were there for; but, that if you were so unlucky as to lay hands on him, you would rot alive. It seems that has been tried out Stanhope way; a man did but give him a blow, and his arm was stiff next day, and he never used it again; and next his hair fell off his head, and then his eyes they turned to water and ran all out of him, and he died within the twelve-month."

Country folk were nearly, though not quite, as superstitious at that time as in the middle ages. "Murrain on him," said Leicester. "Catch me laying a finger on him. I'm glad he is gone; and I hope he won't never come back no more."

"Not likely, since he can read all our hearts. Why, he told me something about you, Tom Leicester; he says you are in love."

"No! did he really now?" and Leicester opened his eyes very wide. "And did he tell you who the lass is?"

"He did so; and surprised me properly." This with a haughty glance.

Leicester held his tongue and turned red.

"Who is it, mistress?" asked the helper.

"He didn't say I was to tell you, young man."

And with these two pricks of her needle she left them both more or less discomfited, and went to scrutinize and anatomize her mistress's heart with plenty of cunning, but no mercy. She related her own part in the affair very briefly, but dwelt with well-feigned sympathy on the priest's feelings. "He turned as white as a sheet, ma'am, when I told him, and offered me his very ring off his finger, he was so grateful; poor man!"

"You did not take it, I hope?" said Mrs. Gaunt, quickly.

"La, no, ma'am. I hadn't the heart."

Mrs. Gaunt was silent awhile. When she spoke again it was to inquire whether Ryder had given him the letter.

"That I did: and it brought the tears into his poor eyes; and such beautiful eyes as he has, to be sure. You would have pitied him if you had seen him read it, and cry over it, and then kiss it and put it in his bosom he did."

Mrs. Gaunt said nothing, but turned her head away.

The operator shot a sly glance into the looking-glass, and saw a pearly tear trickling down her subject's fair cheek. So she went on, all sympathy outside, and remorselessness within. "To think of that face, more like an angel's than a man's, to be dragged through a nasty horse-pond. 'Tis a shame of master to set his men on a clergyman." And so was proceeding, with well-acted and catching warmth, to dig as dangerous a pit for Mrs.

Gaunt as ever was dug for any lady; for whatever Mrs. Gaunt had been betrayed into saying, this Ryder would have used without mercy, and with diabolical skill.

Yes it was a pit, and the lady's pure, but tender heart pushed her towards it, and her fiery temper drew her towards it.

Yet she escaped it this time. The dignity, delicacy, and pride, that is oftener found in these old families than out of them, saved her from that peril. She did not see the trap; but she spurned the bait by native instinct.

She threw up her hand in a moment, with a queenly gesture, and stopped the tempter.

"Not-one-word-from my servant against my husband in my hearing!" said she superbly.

And Ryder shrank back into herself directly.

"Child," said Mrs. Gaunt, "you have done me a great service, and my husband too; for, if this dastardly act had been done in his name, he would soon have been heartily ashamed of it and deplored it. Such services can never be quite repaid; but you will find a purse in that drawer with five guineas; it is yours; and, my lavender silk dress, be pleased to wear that about me; to remind me of the good office you have done me. And now, all you can do for me is to leave me; for I am very, very unhappy."

Ryder retired with the spoil, and Mrs. Gaunt leaned her head over her chair, and cried without stint.

After this, no angry words passed between Mr. and Mrs. Gaunt; but something worse, a settled coolness sprung up.

As for Griffith, his cook kept her place, and the priest came no more to the Castle; so, having outwardly gained the day, he was ready to forget and forgive; but Kate, though she would not let her servant speak ill of Griffith, was deeply indignant and disgusted with him. She met his advances with such a stern coldness, that he turned sulky and bitter in his turn.

Husband and wife saw little of each other, and hardly spoke.

Both were unhappy; but Kate was angriest, and Griffith saddest.

In an evil hour he let out his grief to Caroline Ryder. She seized the opportunity and, by a show of affectionate sympathy and zeal, made herself almost necessary to him, and contrived to establish a very perilous relation between him and her. Matters went so far as this, that the poor man's eye used to brighten when he saw her coming.

Yet this victory cost her a sore heart and all the patient self-denial of her sex. To be welcome to Griffith she had to speak to him of her rival, and to speak well of her. She tried talking of herself and her attachment; he yawned in her face: she tried smooth detraction and innuendo; he fired up directly and defended her, of whose conduct he had been complaining the very moment before.

Then she saw that there was but one way to the man's heart. Sore, and sick, and smiling, she took that way: resolving to bide her time; to worm herself in anyhow, and wait patiently till she could venture to thrust her mistress out.

If any of my readers need to be told why this she-Machiavel threw her fellow conspirators over, the reason was simply this: on calm reflection she saw it was not her interest to get Father Leonard insulted. She looked on him as her mistress's lover, and her own best friend. "Was I mad?" said she to herself. "My business is to keep him sweet upon her, till they can't live without one another: and then I'll tell him; and take your place in this house, my lady."

And now it is time to visit that extraordinary man, who was the cause of all this mischief; whom Gaunt called a villain, and Mrs. Gaunt a saint; and, as usual, he was neither one nor the other.

Father Leonard was a pious, pure, and noble-minded man, who had undertaken to defy nature with religion's aid; and, after years of successful warfare, now sustained one of those defeats to which such warriors have been liable in every age. If his heart was pure, it was tender; and nature never intended him to live all his days alone. After years of prudent coldness to the other sex, he fell in with a creature that put him off his guard at first, she seemed so angelic. "At Wisdom's gate Suspicion slept;" and, by degrees, which have been already indicated in this narrative, she whom the Church had committed to his spiritual care, became his idol. Could he have foreseen this, it would never have happened; he would have steeled himself, or left the country that contained this sweet temptation. But love stole on him, masked with religious zeal, and robed in a garment of light that seemed celestial.

When the mask fell, it was too late: the power to resist the soft and thrilling enchantment was gone. The solitary man was too deep in love.

Yet he clung still to that self-deception, without which he never could have been entrapped into an earthly passion: he never breathed a word of love to her. It would have alarmed her; it would have alarmed himself. Every syllable that passed between these two might have been published without scandal. But the heart does not speak by words alone: there are looks, and there are tones of voice that belong to love, and are his signs, his weapons; and it was in these very tones the priest murmured to his gentle listener about "the angelic life" between spirits still lingering on earth, but purged from earthly dross; and even about other topics less captivating to the religious imagination. He had persuaded her to found a school in this dark parish, and in it he taught the poor with exemplary and touching patience. Well, when he spoke to her about this school, it was in words of practical good sense, but in tones of love; and she, being one of those feminine women who catch the tone they are addressed in, and instinctively answer in tune, and, moreover, seeing no ill but good in the subject of their conversation, replied sometimes, unguardedly enough, in accents almost as tender.

In truth, if Love was really a personage, as the heathens feigned, he must have often perched on a tree, in that quiet grove, and chuckled and mocked, when this man and woman sat and murmured together, in the soft seducing twilight, about the love of God.

And now things had come to a crisis. Husband and wife went about the house silent and gloomy, the ghosts of their former selves; and the priest sat solitary, benighted, bereaved of the one human creature he cared for. Day succeeded to day, and still she never came. Every morning he said, "She will come to-day," and brightened with the hope. But the leaden hours crept by and still she came not.

Three sorrowful weeks went by; and he fell into deep dejection. He used to wander out at night, and come and stand where he could see her windows with the moon shining on them: then go slowly home, cold in body, and with his heart aching, lonely, deserted, and perhaps forgotten. Oh, never till now had he known the utter aching sense of being quite alone in this weary world.

One day, as he sat, drooping and listless, there came a light foot along the passage, a light tap at the door, and, the next moment, she stood before him, a little paler than usual, but lovelier than ever, for celestial pity softened her noble features.

The priest started up with a cry of joy that ought to have warned her; but it only brought a faint blush of pleasure to her cheek and the brimming tears to her eyes.

"Dear father and friend," said she. "What! have you missed me? Think, then, how I have missed you. But 'twas best for us both to let their vile passions cool first."

Leonard could not immediately reply. The emotion of seeing her again so suddenly almost choked him.

He needed all the self-possession he had been years acquiring not to throw himself at her knees and declare his passion to her.

Mrs. Gaunt saw his agitation, but did not interpret it aright.

She came eagerly and sat on a stool beside him. "Dear father," she said, "do not let their insolence grieve you. They have smarted for it, and shall smart till they make their submission to you, and beg and entreat you to come to us again. Meantime, since you cannot visit me, I visit you. Confess me, father, and then direct me with your counsels. Ah! if you could but give me the Christian temper to carry them out firmly but meekly! 'Tis my ungoverned spirit hath wrought all this mischief, mea culpa! mea culpa!"

By this time Leonard had recovered his self-possession, and he spent an hour of strange intoxication, confessing his idol, sentencing his idol to light penances, directing and advising his idol, and all in the soft murmurs of a lover.

She left him and the room seemed to darken.

Two days only elapsed, and she came again. Visit succeeded to visit: and her affection seemed boundless.

The insult he had received was to be avenged in one place, and healed in another, and if possible, effaced with tender hand.

So she kept all her sweetness for that little cottage, and all her acidity for Hernshaw Castle.

It was an evil hour when Griffith attacked her saint with violence. The woman was too high-spirited, and too sure of her own rectitude, to endure that: so, instead of crushing her, it drove her to retaliation; and to imprudence.

These visits to console Father Leonard were quietly watched by Ryder, for one thing. But, worse than that, they placed Mrs. Gaunt in a new position with Leonard, and one that melts the female heart. She was now the protectress and the consoler of a man she admired and revered. I say if any thing on earth can breed love in a grand female bosom, this will.

She had put her foot on a sunny slope clad with innocent-looking flowers; but more and more precipitous at every step, and perdition at the bottom.

CHAPTER IX

Father Leonard, visited, soothed, and petted by his idol, recovered his spirits, and, if he pined during her absence, he was always so joyful in her presence that she thought of course he was permanently happy; so then, being by nature magnanimous and placable, she began to smile on her husband again, and a tacit reconciliation came about by natural degrees.

But this produced a startling result.

Leonard, as her confessor, had only to follow precedents, and ask questions his Church has printed for the use of confessors, and he soon learned enough to infer that their disunion had given way.

The consequence was that one day, being off his guard, or literally unable to contain his bursting heart any longer, he uttered a cry of jealous agony, and then in a torrent of burning, melting words, appealed to her pity. He painted her husband's happiness, and his own misery, and barren desolation, with a fervid passionate eloquence that paralysed his hearer, and left her pale and trembling, and the tears of pity trickling down her cheek.

Those silent tears calmed him a little; and he begged her forgiveness, and awaited his doom.

"I pity you," said she, angelically. "What? you jealous of my husband! Oh, pray to Christ and our Lady to cure you of this folly."

She rose, fluttering inwardly, but calm as a statue on the outside, gave him her hand, and went home very slowly; and the moment she was out of his sight she drooped her head like a crushed flower.

She was sad, ashamed, alarmed.

Her mind was in a whirl; and, were I to imitate those writers who undertake to dissect and analyse the heart at such moments, and put the exact result on paper, I should be apt to sacrifice truth to precision; I must stick to my old plan, and tell you what she did: that will surely be some index to her mind, especially with my female readers.

She went home straight to her husband; he was smoking his pipe after dinner. She drew her chair close to him, and laid her hand tenderly on his shoulder. "Griffith," she said, "will you grant your wife a favour? You once promised to take me abroad: I desire to go now: I long to see foreign countries: I am tired of this place. I want a change. Prithee, prithee take me hence this very day."

Griffith looked aghast. "Why, sweetheart, it takes a deal of money to go abroad; we must get in our rents first."

"Nay, I have a hundred pounds laid by."

"Well, but what a fancy to take all of a sudden!"

"Oh, Griffith, don't deny me what I ask you, with my arm round your neck, dearest. It is no fancy. I want to be alone with you, far from this place where coolness has come between us." And with this she fell to crying and sobbing, and straining him tight to her bosom, as if she feared to lose him, or be taken from him.

Griffith kissed her, and told her to cheer up, he was not the man to deny her anything. "Just let me get my hay in," said he, "and I'll take you to Rome, if you like."

"No, no: to-day, or to-morrow at furthest, or you don't love me as I deserve to be loved by you this day."

"Now Kate, my darling, be reasonable. I must get my hay in; and then I am your man."

Mrs. Gaunt had gradually sunk almost to her knees. She now started up with nostrils expanding and her blue eyes glittering. "Your hay!" she cried, with bitter contempt; "your hay before your wife? That is how you love me."

And, the next moment, she seemed to turn from a fiery woman to a glacier.

Griffith smiled at all this with that lordly superiority the male of our species sometimes wears when he is behaving like a dull ass; and smoked his pipe, and resolved to indulge her whim as soon as ever he had got his hay in.

CHAPTER X

Showery weather set in, and the hay had to be turned twice, and left in cocks instead of carried.

Griffith spoke now and then about the foreign tour; but Kate deigned no reply whatever; and the chilled topic died out before the wet hay could be got in: and so much for Procrastination.

Meantime, Betty Gough was sent for to mend the house-linen. She came every other day after dinner, and sat working alone beside Mrs. Gaunt till dark.

Caroline Ryder put her own construction on this, and tried to make friends with Mrs. Gough, intending to pump her. But Mrs. Gough gave her short, dry answers. Ryder then felt sure that Gough was a go-between, and, woman-like, turned up her nose at her with marked contempt. For why? This office of go-between was one she especially coveted for herself under the circumstances; and, a little while ago, it had seemed within her grasp.

One fine afternoon the hay was all carried, and Griffith came home in good spirits to tell his wife he was ready to make the grand tour with her.

He was met at the gate by Mrs. Gough, with a face of great concern; she begged him to come and see the Dame; she had slipped on the oak stairs, poor soul, and hurt her back.

Griffith tore up the stairs, and found Kate in the drawing-room lying on a sofa, and her doctor by her side. He came in, trembling like a leaf, and clasped her piteously in his arms. At this she uttered a little patient sigh of pain, and the doctor begged him to moderate himself: there was no immediate cause of alarm; but she must be kept quiet: she had strained her back, and her nerves were shaken by the fall.

"Oh, my poor Kate!" cried Griffith; and would let nobody else touch her. She was no longer a tall girl, but a statuesque woman; yet he carried her in his herculean arms up to her bed. She turned her head towards him and shed a gentle tear at this proof of his love; but the next moment she was cold again, and seemed weary of her life.

An invalid's bed was sent to her by the doctor at her own request, and placed on a small bed-stead. She lay on this at night, and on a sofa by day.

Griffith was now as good as a widower; and Caroline Ryder improved the opportunity. She threw herself constantly in his way, all smiles, small talk, and geniality.

Like many healthy men, your sickness wearied him if it lasted over two days; and, whenever he came out, chilled and discontented, from his invalid wife, there was a fine, buoyant, healthy young woman, ready to chat with him, and brimming over with undisguised admiration.

True, she was only a servant; a servant to the core. But she had been always about ladies, and could wear their surface as readily as she could their gowns. Moreover, Griffith himself lacked dignity and reserve: he would talk to anybody.

The two women began to fill the relative situations of clouds, and sunshine.

But, ere this had lasted long, the enticing contact with the object of her lawless fancy inflamed Ryder, and made her so impatient that she struck her long meditated blow a little prematurely.

The passage outside Mrs. Gaunt's door had a large window: and one day, while Griffith was with his wife, Ryder composed herself on the window-seat in a forlorn attitude, too striking and unlike her usual gay demeanour to pass unnoticed.

Griffith came out and saw this drooping disconsolate figure. "Hallo!" said he, "what is wrong with you?" a little fretfully.

A deep sigh was the only response.

"Had words with your sweetheart?"

"You know I have no sweetheart, sir."

The good-natured Squire made an attempt or two to console her and find out what was the matter; but he could get nothing out of her but monosyllables and sighs. At last the crocodile contrived to cry. And having thus secured his pity, she said——

"There, never heed me. I'm a foolish woman; I can't bear to see my dear master so abused."

"What d'ye mean?" said Griffith, sternly. Her very first shaft wounded his peace of mind.

"Oh, no matter! why should I be your friend and my own enemy? If I tell you I shall lose my place."

"Nonsense, girl, you shall never lose your place while I am here."

"Well, I hope not, sir; for I am very happy here; too happy methinks, when you speak kindly to me. Take no notice of what I said. 'Tis best to be blind at times."

The simple Squire did not see that this artful creature was playing the stale game of her sex: stimulating his curiosity under pretence of putting him off. Ho began to fret with suspicion and curiosity, and insisted on her speaking out.

"Ah! but I am so afraid you will hate me," said she; "and that will be worse than losing my place."

Griffith stamped on the ground. "What is it?" said he, fiercely.

Ryder seemed frightened. "It is nothing," said she; then she paused, and added, "but my folly. I can't bear to see you waste your feelings. She is not so ill as you fancy."

"Do you mean to say that my wife is pretending?"

"How can I say that? I wasn't there: nobody saw her fall; nor heard her either; and the house full of people. No doubt there is something the matter with her; but I do believe her heart is in more trouble than her back."

"And what troubles her heart? Tell me, and she shall not fret long."

"Well, sir: then just you send for Father Leonard: and she will get up, and walk as she used, and smile on you as she used. That man is the main of her sickness, you take my word."

Griffith turned sick at heart: and the strong man literally staggered at this envenomed thrust of a weak woman's tongue. But he struggled with the poison.

"What d'ye mean, woman?" said he. "The priest hasn't been near her these two months."

"That is it, sir," replied Eyder, quietly; "he is too wise to come here against your will; and she is bitter against you for frightening him away. Ask yourself, sir, didn't she change to you the moment that you threatened that Leonard with the horse-pond?"

"That is true!" gasped the wretched husband. Yet he struggled again. "But she made it up with me after that. Why, 'twas but the other day she begged me to go abroad with her, and take her away from this place."

"Ah? indeed!" said Ryder, bending her black brows, "did she so?"

"That she did," said Griffith, joyfully: "so you see you are mistaken."

"You should have taken her at her word, sir," was all the woman's reply.

"Well, you see the hay was out: so I put it off; and then came the cursed rain day after day; and so she cooled upon it."

"Of course she did, sir." Then, with a solemnity that appalled her miserable listener, "I'd give all I'm worth if you had taken her at her word that minute. But that is the way with you gentlemen: you let the occasion slip: and we that be women never forgive that: she won't give you the same chance again, I know. Now if I was not afraid to make you unhappy, I'd tell you why she asked you to go abroad. She felt herself weak and saw her danger; she found she could not resist that Leonard any longer; and she had the sense to see it wasn't worth her while to ruin herself for him; so she asked you to save her from him: that is the plain English. And you didn't."

At this Griffith's face wore an expression of agony so horrible that Ryder hesitated in her course. "There, there," said she, "pray don't look so, dear master! after all, there's nothing certain; and perhaps I am too severe where I see you ill-treated: and to be sure no woman could be cold to you unless she was bewitched out of her seven senses by some other man. I couldn't use you as mistress does; but then there's nobody I care a straw for in these parts, except my dear master."

Griffith took no notice of this overture: the potent poison of jealousy was coursing through all his veins and distorting his ghastly face.

"Oh, God!" he gasped, "can this thing be? My wife! the mother of my child! It is a lie! I can't believe it; I won't believe it. Have pity on me, woman, and think again, and unsay your words; for, if 'tis so, there will be murder in this house."

Ryder was alarmed. "Don't talk so," said she, hastily; "no woman born is worth that: besides, as you say, what do we know against her? She is a gentlewoman, and well brought up. Now, dear master, you have got one friend in this house, and that is me: I know women better than you do. Will you be ruled by me?"

"Yes, I will: for I do believe you care a little for me."

"Then don't you believe anything against our Dame. Keep quiet till you know more. Don't you be so simple as to accuse her to her face, or you'll never learn the truth. Just you watch her quietly, without seeming: and I'll help you. Be a man, and know the truth."

"I will!" said Griffith, grinding his teeth. "And I believe she will come out pure as snow."

"Well, I hope so too," said Ryder, drily. Then she added, "But don't you be seen speaking to me too much, sir, or she will suspect me, and then she will be on her guard with me. When I have anything particular to tell you, I'll cough, so; and then I'll run out into the Grove: nobody goes there now."

Griffith did not see the hussy was contriving a series of assignations. He fell into the trap bodily.

The life this man led was now infernal.

He watched his wife night and day to detect her heart; he gave up hunting, he deserted the "Red Lion;" if he went out of doors, it was but a step; he hovered about the place to see if messages came or went; and he spent hours in his wife's bedroom, watching her, grim, silent, and sombre, to detect her inmost heart. His flesh wasted visibly, and his ruddy colour paled. Hell was in his heart. Ay, two hells: jealousy and suspense.

Mrs. Gaunt saw directly that something was amiss, and ere long she divined what it was.

But, if he was jealous, she was proud as Lucifer. So she met his ever-watchful eye with the face of a marble statue.

Only in secret her heart quaked and yearned, and she shed many a furtive tear, and was sore, sore perplexed.

Meantime Ryder was playing with her master's anguish like a cat with a mouse.

Upon the pretence of some petty discovery or other, she got him ou day after day into the Grove, and, to make him believe in her candour and impartiality, would give him feeble reasons for thinking his wife loved him still; taking care to overpower these reasons with some little piece of strong good sense and subtle observation.

It is the fate of moral poisoners to poison themselves as well as thei victims. This is a just retribution, and it fell upon this female Iago. He wretched master now loved his wife to distraction, yet hated her to the death: and Ryder loved her master passionately, yet hated him intensely by fits and starts.

These secret meetings on which she had counted so, what did she gai by them? She saw that, with all her beauty, intelligence, and zeal for him she was nothing to him still. He suspected, he sometimes hated his wife but he was always full of her. There was no getting any other wedge int his heart.

This so embittered Ryder that one day she revenged herself on him.

He had been saying that no earthly torment could equal his: all hi watching had shown him nothing for certain. "Oh," said he, "if I could onl get proof of her innocence, or proof of her guilt! Anything better than th misery of doubt. It gnaws my heart, it consumes my flesh. I can't sleep, I can't eat, I can't sit down. I envy the dead that lie at peace. Oh, my heart! my heart!"

"And all for a woman that is not young, nor half so handsome as yourself. Well, sir, I'll try and cure you of your doubt, if that is what torments you. When you threatened that Leonard, he got his orders to come here no more. But she visited him at his place again and again."

"'Tis false! How know you that?"

"As soon as your back was turned she used to order her horse and ride to him."

"How do you know she went to him?"

"I mounted the tower, and saw the way she took."

Griffith's face was a piteous sight, he stammered out, "Well, he is her confessor. She always visited him at times."

"Ay, sir; but in those days her blood was cool, and his too; but bethink you now, when you threatened the man with the horse-pond, he became your enemy. All revenge is sweet; but what revenge is so sweet to any man as that which came to his arms of its own accord? I do notice that men can't read men, but any woman can read a woman. Maids they are reserved, because their mothers have told them that is the only way to get married. But what have a wife and a priest to keep them distant? Can they ever hope to come together lawfully? That is why a priest's light-o'-love is always some honest man's wife. What had those two to keep them from folly? Old Betty Gough? Why, the mistress had bought her, body and soul, long ago. No, sir, you had no friend there; and you had three enemies—love, revenge, and opportunity. Why, what did the priest say to me? I met him not ten yards from here. 'Ware the horse-pond!' says I. Says he, 'Since I am to have the bitter, I'll have the sweet as well.'"[1]

These infernal words were not spoken in vain. Griffith's features were horribly distorted, his eyes rolled fearfully, and he fell to the ground, grinding his teeth, and foaming at the mouth. An epileptic fit!

[1]Compare this statement with p. 129.

Ah epileptic fit is a terrible sight: the simple description of one in our medical books is appalling.

And in this case it was all the more fearful, the subject being so strong and active.

Caroline Ryder shrieked with terror, but no one heard her; at all events, no one came; to be sure the place had a bad name for ghosts, etc.

She tried to hold his head, but could not, for his body kept bounding from the earth with inconceivable elasticity and fury, and his arms flew in every direction; and presently Ryder received a violent blow that almost stunned her.

She lay groaning and trembling beside the victim of her poisonous tongue and of his own passion.

When she recovered herself he was snorting rather than breathing, but lying still and pale enough, his eyes set and glassy.

She got up, and went with uneven steps to a little rill hard by, and plunged her face in it: then filled her beaver hat, and came and dashed water repeatedly in his face.

He came to his senses by degrees; but was weak as an infant. Then Ryder wiped the foam from his lips, and kneeling on her knees, laid a soft hand upon his heavy head, shedding tears of pity and remorse, and sick at heart herself.

For what had she gained by blackening her rival? The sight of his bodily agony, and his ineradicable love.

Mrs. Gaunt sat out of shot, cold, calm, superior.

Yet, in the desperation of her passion, it was something to nurse his "weak head an instant and shed hot tears upon his brow; it was a positive joy, and soon proved a fresh and inevitable temptation.

"My poor master," said she, tenderly, "I never will say a word to you again. It is better to be blind. My God! how you cling to her that feigns a broken back to be rid of you, when there are others as well to look at, and ever so much younger, that adore every hair on your head, and would follow you round the world for one kind look."

"Let no one love me like that," said Griffith, feebly, "to love so, is to be miserable."

"Pity her then, at least," murmured Ryder; and, feeling she had quite committed herself now, her bosom panted under Griffith's ear, and told him the secret she had kept till now.

My female readers will sneer at this temptation: my male readers know that scarcely one man out of a dozen, sick, sore, and hating her he loved, would have turned away from the illicit consolation thus offered to him in his hour of weakness with soft seducing tones, warm tears, and heart that panted at his ear.

CHAPTER XI

How did poor, faulty Griffith receive it?

He raised his head, and turned his brown eye gentle but full upon her. "My poor girl," said he, "I see what you are driving at. But that will not do. I have nothing to give you in exchange. I hate my wife that I loved so dear: d—n her! d—n her! But I hate all womankind for her sake. Keep you clear of me. I would ruin no poor girl for heartless sport. I shall have blood on my hands ere long, and that is enough."

And, with these alarming words, he seemed suddenly to recover all his vigour; for he rose and stalked away at once, and never looked behind him.

Ryder made no further attempt. She sat down and shed bitter tears of sorrow and mortification.

After this cruel rebuff she must hate somebody; and with the justice of her sex, she pitched on Mrs. Gaunt, and hated her like a demon, and watched to do her a mischief by hook or by crook.

Griffith's appearance and manner caused Mrs. Gaunt very serious anxiety. His clothes hung loose on his wasted frame; his face was of one uniform sallow tint, like a maniac's; and he sat silent for hours beside his wife, eyeing her askant from time to time like a surly mastiff guarding some treasure.

She divined what was passing in his mind, and tried to soothe him; but almost in vain. He was sometimes softened for the moment; but hæret lateri lethalis arundo; he still hovered about, watching her and tormenting himself; gnawed mad by three vultures of the mind—doubt, jealousy and suspense.

Then Mrs. Gaunt wrote letters to Father Leonard: hitherto she had only sent him short messages.

Betty Gough carried these letters and brought the answers.

Griffith, thanks to the hint Ryder had given him, suspected this, and waylaid the old woman, and roughly demanded to see the letter she was carrying. She stoutly protested she had none. He seized her, turned her pockets inside out, and found a bunch of keys; item, a printed dialogue between Peter and Herod, omitted in the canonical books, but described by the modern discoverer as an infallible charm for the toothache; item, a brass thimble; item, half a nutmeg.

"Curse your cunning," said he; and went off muttering.

The old woman tottered trembling to Mrs. Gaunt, related this outrage with an air of injured innocence, then removed her cap, undid her hair, and took out a letter from Leonard.

"This must end, and shall," said Mrs. Gaunt, firmly; "else it will drive him mad and me too." Bolton fair-day came. It was a great fair, and had attractions for all classes. There were cattle and horses of all kinds for sale, and also shows, games, wrestling, and dancing till day-break.

All the servants had a prescriptive right to go to this fair: and Griffith himself had never missed one. He told Kate over-night he would go, if it were not for leaving her alone.

The words were kinder than their meaning; but Mrs. Gaunt had the tact, or the candour, to take them in their best sense. "And I would go with you, my dear," said she; "but I should only be a drag. Never heed me; give yourself a day's pleasure, for indeed you need it. I am in care about you: you are so dull of late."

"Well, I will," said Griffith. "I'll not mope here when all the rest are merry-making."

Accordingly, next day about eleven in the morning, he mounted his horse and rode to the fair, leaving the house empty; for all the servants were gone except the old housekeeper; she was tied to the fireside by rheumatics. Even Ryder started, with a new bonnet and red ribbons; but that was only a blind. She slipped back and got unperceived into her own bedroom.

Griffith ran through the fair; but could not enjoy it. Hærebat lateri arundo. He came galloping back to watch his wife, and see whether Betty Gough had come again or not.

As he rode into the stable-yard he caught sight of Ryder's face at an upper window. She looked pale and agitated, and her black eyes flashed with a strange expression. She made him a signal which he did not understand; but she joined him directly after in the stable-yard.

"Come quietly with me," said she, solemnly.

He hooked his horse's rein to the wall, and followed her, trembling.

She took him up the back stairs, and, when she got on the landing, she turned and said, "Where did you leave her?"

"In her own room."

"See if she is there now," said Ryder, pointing to the door.

Griffith tore the door open: the room was empty.

"Nor is she to be found in the house," said Ryder; "for I've been in every room."

Griffith's face turned livid, and he staggered and leaned against the wall. "Where is she?" said he, hoarsely.

"Humph!" said Ryder, fiendishly. "Find him, and you will find her."

"I'll find them if they are above ground," cried Griffith, furiously; and he rushed into his bedroom and soon came out again, with a fearful purpose written on his ghastly features and in his bloodshot eyes; and a loaded pistol in his hand.

Ryder was terrified; but instead of succumbing to terror, she flew at him like a cat and wreathed her arms round him.

"What would you do?" cried she. "Madman, would you hang for them? and break my heart; the only woman in the world that loves you. Give me the pistol. Nay, I will have it."

And, with that extraordinary power excitement lends her sex, she wrenched it out of his hands.

He gnashed his teeth with fury, and clutched her with a gripe of iron: she screamed with pain: he relaxed his grasp a little at that: she turned on him and defied him.

"I won't let you get into trouble for a priest and a wanton," she cried; "you shall kill me first. Leave mo the pistol, and pledge me your sacred word to do them no harm, and then I'll tell you where they are. Refuse me this, and you shall go to your grave and know nothing more than you know now."

"No, no: if you are a woman have pity on me; let me come at them. There, I'll use no weapon. I'll tear them to atoms with these hands. Where are they?"

"May I put the pistol away, then?"

"Yes, take it out of my sight; so best. Where are they?"

Ryder locked the pistol up in one of Mrs. Gaunt's boxes. Then she said, in a trembling voice, "Follow me."

He followed her in awful silence.

She went rather slowly to the door that opened on the lawn; and then she hesitated. "If you are a man, and have any feeling for a poor girl who loves you; if you are a gentleman, and respect your word—no violence."

"I promise," said he. "Where are they?"

"Nay, nay. I fear I shall rue the day I told you. Promise me once more: no bloodshed—upon your soul."

"I promise. Where are they?"

"God forgive me; they are in the Grove."

He bounded away from her like some beast of prey; and she crouched and trembled on the steps of the door: and, now that she realized what she was doing, a sickening sense of dire misgiving came over her and made her feel quite faint.

And so the weak, but dangerous creature sat crouching and quaking, and launched the strong one.

Griffith was soon in the Grove; and the first thing he saw was Leonard and his wife walking together in earnest conversation. Their backs were towards him. Mrs. Gaunt, whom he had left lying on a sofa, and who professed herself scarce able to walk half a dozen times across the room, was now springing along, elastic as a young greyhound, and full of fire and animation. The miserable husband saw, and his heart died within him.

He leaned against a tree and groaned.

The deadly sickness of his heart soon gave way to sombre fury. He came softly after them, with ghastly cheek, and bloodthirsty eyes, like red-hot coals.

They stopped; and he heard his wife say, "'Tis a solemn promise, then: this very night." The priest bowed assent. Then they spoke in so low a voice, he could not hear; but his wife pressed a purse upon Leonard, and Leonard hesitated, but ended by taking it.

Griffith uttered a yell like a tiger, and rushed between them with savage violence, driving the lady one way with his wrists, and the priest another. She screamed: he trembled in silence.

Griffith stood a moment between these two pale faces, silent and awful.

Then he faced his wife. "You vile wretch!" he cried: "so you buy your own dishonour, and mine." He raised his hand high over her head; she never winced. "Oh! but for my oath, I'd lay you dead at my feet. But no; I'll not hang for a priest and a wanton. So, this is the thing you love, and pay it to love you." And with all the mad inconsistency of rage, which mixes small things and great, he tore the purse out of Leonard's hand: then seized him felly by the throat.

At that the high spirit of Mrs. Gaunt gave way to abject terror. "Oh, mercy! mercy!" she cried; "it is all a mistake." And she clung to his knees.

He spurned her furiously away. "Don't touch me, woman," he cried, "or you are dead. Look at this!" And in a moment, with gigantic strength and fury, he dashed the priest down at her feet. "I know ye, ye proud devil," he cried, "love the thing you have seen me tread upon! love it—if ye can." And he literally trampled upon the poor priest with both feet.

Leonard shrieked for mercy.

"None, in this world or the next," roared Griffith; but the next moment he took fright at himself. "God!" he cried, "I must go, or kill. Live and be damned for ever, the pair of ye." And with this he fled from them, grinding his teeth and beating the air with his clenched lists.

He darted to the stable-yard, sprang on his horse, and galloped away from Hernshaw Castle, with the face, the eyes, the gestures, the incoherent mutterings of a raving Bedlamite.

CHAPTER XII

At the fair the wrestling was ended, and the tongues going over it all again, and throwing the victors; the greasy pole, with leg of mutton attached by ribbons, was being hoisted, and the swings flying, and the lads and lasses footing it to the fife and tabor, and the people chattering in groups; when the clatter of a horse's feet was heard, and a horseman burst in and rode recklessly through the market-place; indeed, if his noble horse had been as rash as he was, some would have been trampled under foot. The rider's face was ghastly: such as were not exactly in his path, had time to see it, and wonder how this terrible countenance came into that merry place. Thus, as he passed, shouts of dismay arose, and a space opened before him, and then closed behind him with a great murmur that followed at his heels.

Tom Leicester was listening, spell-bound, on the outskirts of the throng, to the songs and humorous tirades of a pedlar selling his wares; and was saying to himself, "I too will be a pedlar." Hearing the row, he turned round, and saw his master just coming down with that stricken face.

Tom could not decipher his own name in print or manuscript; and these are the fellows that beat us all at reading countenances: he saw in a moment that some great calamity had fallen on Griffith's head; and nature stirred in him. He darted to his master's side, and seized the bridle. "What is up?" he cried.

But Griffith did not answer, nor notice; his ears were almost deaf, and his eyes, great and staring, were fixed right ahead; and to all appearance, he did not see the people: he seemed to be making for the horizon.

"Master! for the love of Heaven, speak to me," cried Leicester. "What have they done to you? Whither be you going, with the face of a ghost?"

"Away, from the hangman," shrieked Griffith, still staring at the horizon. "Stay me not; my hands itch for their throats; my heart thirsts for their blood; but I'll not hang for a priest and a wanton." Then he suddenly turned on Leicester, "Let thou go, or— —," and he lifted up his heavy riding whip.

Then Leicester let go the rein, and the whip descended on the horse's flank; he went clattering furiously over the stones, and drove the thinner groups apart like chaff, and his galloping feet were soon heard fainter and fainter till they died away in the distance. Leicester stood gaping.

Griffith's horse, a black hunter of singular power and beauty, carried his wretched master well that day; he went on till sunset, trotting, cantering, and walking, without intermission; the whip ceased to touch him, the rein never checked him. He found he was the master, and he went his own way. He took his broken rider back into the county where he had been foaled. But a few miles from his native place they came to the "Packhorse," a pretty little roadside inn, with farm-yard and buildings at the back. He had often baited here in his infancy; and now, stiff and stumbling with fatigue, the good horse could not pass the familiar place; he walked gravely into the stable-yard, and there fairly came to an end; craned out his drooping head, crooked his limbs, and seemed of wood. And no wonder. He was ninety-three miles from his last corn.

Paul Carrick, a young farrier, who frequented the "Packhorse," happened just then to be lounging at the kitchen door, and saw him come in. He turned directly, and shouted into the house, "Ho! Master Vint, come hither. Here's Black Dick come home, and brought you a worshipful customer."

The landlord bustled out of the kitchen, crying, "They are welcome both." Then he came lowly louting to Griffith, cap in hand, and held the horse, poor immoveable brute; and his wife curtsied perseveringly at the door.

Griffith dismounted, and stood there looking like one in a dream.

"Please you come in, sir," said the landlady, smiling professionally

He followed her mechanically.

"Would your worship be private? We keep a parlour for gentles."

"Ay, let me be alone," he groaned.

Mercy Vint, the daughter, happened to be on the stairs and heard him: the voice startled her, and she turned round directly to look at the speaker; but she only saw his back going into the room, and then he flung himself like a sack into the arm-chair.

The landlady invited him to order supper: he declined. She pressed him. He flung a piece of money on the table, and told her savagely to score his supper, and leave him in peace.

She flounced out with a red face, and complained to her husband in the kitchen.

Harry Vint rung the crown piece on the table before he committed himself to a reply. It rang like a bell. "Churl or not, his coin is good," said Harry Vint, philosophically. "I'll eat his supper, dame, for that matter."

"Father," whispered Mercy, "I do think the gentleman is in trouble."

"And that is no business of mine, neither," said Harry Vint.

Presently the guest they were discussing called loudly for a quart of burnt wine.

When it was ready, Mercy offered to take it in to him. She was curious. The landlord looked up rather surprised; for his daughter attended to the farm, but fought shy of the inn and its business.

"Take it, lass, and welcome for me," said Mrs. Vint, pettishly.

Mercy took the wine in, and found Griffith with his head buried in his hands.

She stood a while with the tray, not knowing what to do.

Then, as he did not move, she said, softly, "The wine, sir, an if it please you."

Griffith lifted his head, and turned two eyes clouded with suffering upon her; he saw a buxom, blooming, young woman, with remarkably dove-like eyes that dwelt with timid, kindly curiosity upon him. He looked at her in a half distracted way, and then put his hand to the mug. "Here's perdition to all false women!" said he, and tossed half the wine down at a single draught.

"'Tis not to me you drink, sir," said Mercy, with gentle dignity. Then she curtsied modestly and retired, discouraged, not offended.

The wretched Griffith took no notice—did not even see he had repulsed a friendly visitor. The wine, taken on an empty stomach, soon stupified him, and he staggered to bed.

He awoke at day-break; and, oh the agony of that waking.

He lay sighing a while, with his hot skin quivering on his bones, and his heart like lead; then got up and flung his clothes on hastily, and asked how far to the nearest sea-port.

Twenty miles.

He called for his horse. The poor brute was dead lame.

He cursed that good servant for going lame. He walked round and round like a wild beast, chafing and fuming a while; then sank into a torpor of dejection, and sat with his head bowed on the table all day.

He ate scarcely any food; but drank wine freely, remarking, however, that it was false-hearted stuff; did him no good; and had no taste as wine used to have. "But nothing is what it was," said he. "Even I was happy once. But that seems years ago."

"Alas! poor gentleman; God comfort you," said Mercy Vint, and came with the tears in her dove-like eyes, and said to her father, "To be sure his worship hath been crossed in love; and what could she be thinking of? Such a handsome, well-made gentleman!"

"Now that is a wench's first thought," said Harry Vint: "more likely lost his money, gambling, or racing. But, indeed, I think 'tis his head is disordered, not his heart. I wish the 'Packhorse' was quit of him, maugre his laced coat. We want no kill-joys here."

That night he was heard groaning and talking, and did not come down at all.

So at noon Mrs. Vint knocked at his door: a weak voice bade her enter; she found him shivering, and he asked her for a fire.

She grumbled, out of hearing, but lighted a fire.

Presently his voice was heard hallooing: he wanted all the windows open: he was so burning hot.

The landlady looked at him, and saw his face was flushed and swollen: and he complained of pain in all his bones. She opened the windows, and asked him would he have a doctor sent for: he shook his head contemptuously.

However, towards evening he became delirious, and raved and tossed, and rolled his head as if it was an intolerable weight he wanted to get rid of.

The females of the family were for sending at once for a doctor; but the prudent Harry demurred.

"Tell me, first, who is to pay the fee," said he. "I've seen a fine coat with the pockets empty, before to-day."

The women set up their throats at him with one accord, each after her kind.

"Out, fie!" said Mercy; "are we to do nought for charity?"

"Why, there's his horse, ye foolish man," said Mrs. Vint.

"Ay, ye are both wiser than me," said Harry Vint, ironically. And soon after that he went out softly.

The next minute he was in the sick man's room, examining his pockets. To his infinite surprise he found twenty gold pieces, a quantity of silver, and some trinkets.

He spread them all out on the table and gloated on them with greedy eyes. They looked so inviting, that he said to himself, they would be safer in his custody than in that of a delirious person, who was even now raving incoherently before him, and could not see what he was doing. He therefore proceeded to transfer them to his own care.

On the way to his pocket, his shaking hand was arrested by another hand, soft, but firm as iron. He shuddered and looked round in abject terror; and there was his daughter's face, pale as his own, but full of resolution. "Nay, father," said she; "I must take charge of these: and well do you know why."

These simple words cowed Harry Vint, so that he instantly resigned the money and jewels, and retired, muttering that "things were come to a pretty pass,"—"a man was no longer master in his own house," etc. etc. etc.

While he inveighed against the degeneracy of the age, the women paid him no more attention than the age did, but just sent for the doctor. He came, and bled the patient. This gave him a momentary relief; but when in the natural progress of the disease, sweating and weakness came on, the loss of the precious vital fluid was fatal, and the patient's pulse became scarce perceptible. There he lay, with wet hair, and gleaming eyes, and haggard face, at death's door.

An experienced old crone was got to nurse him, and she told Mrs. Vint he would live maybe three days.

Paul Carrick used to come to the "Packhorse" after Mercy Vint, and, finding her sad, asked her what was the matter.

"What should it be," said she, "but the poor gentleman a-dying overhead; away from all his friends."

"Let me see him," said Paul.

Mercy took him softly into the room.

"Ay, he is booked," said the farrier. "Doctor has taken too much blood out of the man's body. They kill a many that way."

"Alack, Paul! must he die? Can nought be done?" said Mercy, clasping her hands.

"I don't say that, neither," said the farrier. "He is a well-made man: he is young. I might save him, perhaps, if I had not so many beasts to look to. I'll tell you what you do. Make him soup as strong as strong; have him watched night and day, and let 'em put a spoonful of warm wine into him every hour, and then of soup; egg flip is a good thing, too; change his bed-linen, and keep the doctors from him: that is his only chance: he is fairly dying of weakness. But I must be off; Farmer Blake's cow is down for calving: I must give her an ounce of salts before 'tis too late."

Mercy Vint scanned the patient closely, and saw that Paul Carrick was right. She followed his instructions to the letter, with one exception. Instead of trusting to the old woman, of whom she had no very good opinion, she had the great arm-chair brought into the sick-room, and watched the patient herself by night and day: a gentle hand cooled his temples; a gentle hand brought concentrated nourishment to his lips; and a mellow voice coaxed him to be good and swallow it. There are voices it is not natural to resist; and Griffith learned by degrees to obey this one, even when he was half unconscious.

At the end of three days this zealous young nurse thought she discerned a slight improvement, and told her mother so. Then the old lady came and examined the patient, and shook her head gravely. Her judgment, like her daughter's, was influenced by her wishes.

The fact is, both landlord and landlady were now calculating upon Griffith's decease. Harry had told her about the money and jewels, and the pair had put their heads together, and settled that Griffith was a gentleman highwayman, and his spoil would never be reclaimed after his decease, but fall to those good Samaritans, who were now nursing him, and intended to bury him respectably. The future being thus settled, this worthy couple became a little impatient; for Griffith, like Charles the Second, was "an unconscionable time dying."

We order dinner to hasten a lingering guest, and, with equal force of logic, mine host of the "Packhorse" spoke to White, the village carpenter, about a full-sized coffin: and his wife set the old crone to make a linen shroud, unobtrusively, in the bakehouse.

On the third afternoon of her nursing, Mercy left her patient, and called up the crone to tend him. She herself, worn out with fatigue, threw herself on a bed in her mother's room, hard by, and soon fell asleep.

She had slept about two hours when she was wakened by a strange noise in the sick chamber. A man and a woman quarrelling.

She bounded off the bed, and was in the room directly.

Lo and behold, there were the nurse and the dying man abusing one another like pick-pockets.

The cause of this little misunderstanding was not far to seek. The old crone had brought up her work, videlicet, a winding-sheet all but finished, and certain strips of glazed muslin about three inches deep. She soon completed the winding-sheet, and hung it over two chairs in the patient's sight; she then proceeded to double the slips in six, and nick them; then she unrolled them, and they were frills, and well adapted to make the coming corpse absurd, and divest it of any little dignity the King of Terrors might bestow on it.

She was so intent upon her congenial task, that she did not observe the sick man had awakened, and was viewing her and her work with an intelligent but sinister eye.

"What is that you are making?" said he, grimly.

The voice was rather clear, and strong, and seemed so loud and strange in that still chamber, that it startled the woman mightily. She uttered a little shriek, and then was wrath. "Plague take the man!" said she; "how you scared me. Keep quiet, do; and mind your own business," [The business of going off the hooks.]

"I ask you what is that you are making," said Griffith, louder; and raising himself on his arm.

"Baby's frills," replied the woman, coolly, recovering that contempt for the understandings of the dying, which marks the veritable crone.

"Ye lie," said Griffith. "And there is a shroud. Who is that for?"

"Who should it be for, thou simple body? Keep quiet, do, till the change comes. 'Twon't be long now; art too well to last till sun-down."

"So 'tis for me, is it?" screamed Griffith. "I'll disappoint ye yet. Give me my clothes. I'll not lie here to be measured for my grave, ye old witch."

"Here's manners!" cackled the indignant crone. "Ye foul-mouthed knave! is this how you thank a decent woman for making a comfortable corpse of ye, you that has no right to die in your shoes, let a be such dainties as muslin neck-ruff, and shroud of good Dutch flax."

At this Griffith discharged a volley, in which "vulture," "hag," "blood-sucker," etc., blended with as many oaths: during which Mercy came in.

She glided to him, with her dove's eyes full of concern, and laid her hand gently on his shoulder: "You'll work yourself a mischief," said she; "leave me to scold her. Why, my good Nelly, how could you be so hare-brained? prithee take all that trumpery away this minute: none here needeth it, nor shall not this many a year, please God."

"They want me dead," said Griffith to her, piteously, finding he had got one friend: and sunk back on his pillow exhausted.

"So it seems," said Mercy, cunningly. "But I'd baulk them finely. I'd up and order a beef-steak this minute."

"And shall," said Griffith, with feeble spite. "Leastways, do you order it, and I'll eat it:— d——n her!"

Sick men are like children; and women soon find that out, and manage them accordingly. In ten minutes Mercy brought a good rump-steak to the bedside, and said "Now for't. Marry come, up, with her winding-sheets!"

Thus played upon, and encouraged, the great baby ate more than half the steak; and soon after perspired gently, and fell asleep.

Paul Carrick found him breathing gently, with a slight tint of red in his cheek; and told Mercy there was a change for the better. "We have brought him to a true intermission," said he; "so throw in the bark at once."

"What, drench his honour's worship!" said Mercy, innocently. "Nay, send thou the medicine, and I'll find womanly ways to get it down him."

Next day came the doctor, and whispered softly to Mrs. Vint, "How are we all upstairs?"

"Why couldn't you come afore?" replied Mrs Vint, crossly. "Here's farrier Carrick stepped in, and curing him out of hand; the meddlesome body."

"A farrier rob me of my patient!" cried the doctor, in high dudgeon.

"Nay, good sir, 'tis no fault of mine. This Paul is a sort of a kind of a follower of our Mercy's: and she is mistress here, I trow."

"And what hath his farriership prescribed? Friar's balsam, belike."

"Nay, I know not; but you may soon learn, for he is above, physicking the gentleman (a pretty gentleman!) and suiting to our Mercy—after a manner."

The doctor declined to make one in so mixed a consultation.

"Give me my fee, dame," said he: "and as for this impertinent farrier, the patient's blood be on his head; and I'd have him beware the law."

Mrs. Vint went to the stair-foot and screamed, "Mercy, the good doctor wants his fee. Who is to pay it, I wonder?"

"I'll bring it him anon," said a gentle voice: and Mercy soon came down and paid it with a willing air that half disarmed professional fury.

"'Tis a good lass, dame," said the doctor, when she was gone; "and, by the same token, I wish her better mated than to a scrub of a farrier."

Griffith, still weak, but freed of fever, woke one glorious afternoon, and heard a bird-like voice humming a quaint old ditty, and saw a field of golden wheat through an open window, and seated at that window the mellow songstress, Mercy Vint, plying her needle, with lowered lashes but beaming face, a picture of health and quiet womanly happiness. Things were going to her mind in that sick-room.

He looked at her, and at the golden corn and summer haze beyond, and the tide of life seemed to rush back upon him.

"My good lass," said he, "tell me, where am I? for I know not."

Mercy started, and left off singing, then rose and came slowly towards him, with her work in her hand.

Innocent joy at this new symptom of convalescence flushed her comely features, but she spoke low.

"Good sir, at the 'Packhorse,'" said she, smiling. "The 'Packhorse?' and where is that?"

"Hard by Allerton village."

"And where is that? not in Cumberland?"

"Nay, in Lancashire, your worship. Why, whence come you that know not the 'Packhorse,' nor yet Allerton township? Come you from Cumberland?"

"No matter whence I come. I'm going on board ship; like my father before me."

"Alas, sir, you are not fit; you have been very ill; and partly distraught."

She stopped: for Griffith turned his face to the wall with a deep groan. It had all rushed over him in a moment.

Mercy stood still, and worked on, but the water gathered in her eyes at that eloquent groan.

By-and-by Griffith turned round again, with a face of anguish, and filmy eyes, and saw her in the same place standing, working, and pitying.

"What, are you there still?" said he, roughly.

"Ay, sir; but I'll go, sooner than be troublesome. Can I fetch you anything?"

"No. Ay, wine; bring me wine to drown it all."

She brought him a pint of wine.

"Pledge me," said he, with a miserable attempt at a smile.

She put the cup to her lips, and sipped a drop or two; but her dove's eyes were looking up at him over the liquor all the time. Griffith soon disposed of the rest; and asked for more.

"Nay," said she, "but I dare not: the doctor hath forbidden excess in drinking."

"The doctor! what doctor?"

"Doctor Paul," said she, demurely. "He hath saved your life, sir, I do think."

"Plague take him for that!"

"So say not I."

Here she left him with an excuse. "'Tis milking time, sir: and you shall know that I am our dairymaid. I seldom trouble the inn."

Next day she was on the window-seat, working and beaming. The patient called to her in peevish accents to put his head higher. She laid down her work with a smile, and came and raised his head.

"There, now, that is too high," said he: "how awkward you are."

"I lack experience, sir, but not good will. There, now, is that a little better?"

"Ay, a little. I'm sick of lying here: I want to get up. Dost hear what I say? I—want—to get up."

"And so you shall. As soon as ever you are fit. To-morrow, perhaps. To-day, you must e'en be patient. Patience is a rare medicine."

Tic, tic, tic! "What a noise they are making downstairs. Go, lass, and bid them hold their peace."

Mercy shook her head. "Good lack-a-day! we might as well bid the river give over running; but, to be sure, this comes of keeping a hostelry, sir. When we had only the farm, we were quiet, and did no ill to no one."

"Well, sing me, to drown their eternal buzzing: it worries me dead."

"Me sing! alack, sir, I'm no songster."

"That is false. You sing like a throstle. I dote on music; and, when I was delirious, I heard one singing about my bed; I thought it was an angel at that time; but 'twas only you, my young mistress: and now I ask you, you say me nay. That is the way with you all. Plague take the girl, and all her curst, unreasonable, hypocritical sex. I warrant me you'd sing if I wanted to sleep; and dance the devil to a standstill."

Mercy, instead of flouncing out of the room, stood looking on him with maternal eyes, and chuckling like a bird.

"That is right, sir: tax us all to your heart's content. O, but I'm a joyful woman to hear you; for 'tis a sure sign of mending when the sick take to rating of their nurses."

"In sooth, I am too cross-grained," said Griffith, relenting.

"Not a whit, sir, for my taste. I've been in care for you: and now you are a little cross, that maketh me easy."

"Thou art a good soul. Wilt sing me a stave after all?"

"La, you now; how you come back to that. Ay, and with a good heart: for, to be sure, 'tis a sin to gainsay a sick man. But indeed I am the homeliest singer. Methinks 'tis time I went down and bade them cook your worship's supper."

"Nay, I'll not eat nor sup, till I hear thee sing."

"Your will is my law, sir," said Mercy, drily, and retired to the window-seat; that was the first obvious preliminary. Then she fiddled with her apron, and hem'd, and waited in hopes a reprieve might come; but a peevish, relentless voice demanded the song at intervals.

So then she turned her head carefully away from her hearer, lowered her eyes, and, looking the picture of guilt and shame all the time, sang an ancient ditty. The poltroon's voice was rich, mellow, clear, and sweet as honey; and she sang the notes for the sake of the words, not the words for the sake of the notes, as all but Nature's singers do.

The air was grave as well as sweet; for Mercy was of an old Puritan stock, and even her songs were not giddy-paced, but solid, quaint, and tender; all the more did they reach the soul.

In vain was the blushing cheek averted, and the honeyed lips: the ravishing tones set the birds chirping outside, yet filled the room within, and the glasses rang in harmony upon the shelf as the sweet singer poured out from her heart (so it seemed) the speaking song that begins thus——

> In vain you tell your parting lover
> You wish fair winds may waft him over,
>
> Alas, what winds can happy prove
> That bear me far from her I love?

Alas, what dangers on the main
Can equal those that I sustain
From slighted love and cold disdain.

Griffith beat time with his hand awhile, and his own face softened and beautified as the melody curled about his heart. But soon it was too much for him; he knew the song; had sung it to Kate Peyton in their days of courtship. A thousand memories gushed in upon his soul and overpowered him. He burst out sobbing violently, and wept as if his heart must break.

"Alas! what have I done?" said Mercy: and the tears ran swiftly from her eyes at the sight. Then, with native delicacy, she hurried from the room.

What Griffith went through that night, in silence, was never known but to himself. But the next morning he was a changed man. He was all dogged resolution: put on his clothes unaided, though he could hardly stand to do it; and borrowed the landlord's staff, and crawled out a smart distance into the sun. "It was kill or cure," said he. "I am to live, it seems. Well, then, the past is dead. My life begins again to-day."

Hen-like Mercy soon learned this sally of her refractory duckling, and was uneasy. So, for an excuse to watch him, she brought him out his money and jewels, and told him she had thought it safest to take charge of them.

He thanked her cavalierly, and offered her a diamond ring.

She blushed scarlet, and declined it; and even turned a meekly reproachful glance on at him with her dove's eyes.

He had a suit of russet made, and put away his fine coat, and forbade any one to call him "Your worship." "I am a farmer, like yourselves," said he; "and my name is——Thomas Leicester."

A brain fever either kills the unhappy lover, or else benumbs the very anguish that caused it.

And so it was with Griffith. His love got benumbed, and the sense of his wrongs vivid. He nursed a bitter hatred of his wife; only, as he could not punish her without going near her, and no punishment short of death seemed enough for her, he set to work to obliterate her from his very memory, if possible. He tried employment: he pottered about the little farm, advising and helping, and that so zealously that the landlord retired altogether from that department, and Griffith, instead of he, became Mercy's ally, agricultural and bucolical. She was a shepherdess to the core, and hated the poor "Packhorse."

For all that it was her fate to add to its attractions: for Griffith bought a viol da gambo, and taught her sweet songs, which he accompanied with such skill and, sometimes, with his voice, that good company often looked in on the chance of a good song sweetly sung and played.

The sick in body, or mind, are egotistical. Griffith was no exception: bent on curing his own deep wound, he never troubled his head about the wound he might inflict.

He was grateful to his sweet nurse, and told her so. And his gratitude charmed her all the more that it had been rather long in coming.

He found this dove-like creature a wonderful soother: he applied her more and more to his sore heart.

As for Mercy, she had been too good and kind to her patient not to take a tender interest in his convalescence. Our hearts warm more to those we have been kind to, than to those who have been kind to us: and the female reader can easily imagine what delicious feelings stole into that womanly heart, when she saw her pale nursling pick up health and strength under her wing, and become the finest, handsomest man in the parish.

Pity and admiration; where these meet, love is not far behind.

And then this man, who had been cross and rough while he was weak, became gentler, kinder, and more deferential to her, the stronger he got.

Mrs. Vint saw they were both fond of each other's company, and disapproved it. She told Paul Garrick if he had any thought of Mercy he had bettor give over shilly-shallying, for there was another man after her. Paul made light of it at first. "She has known me too long to take up her head with a newcomer," said he. "To be sure I never asked her to name the day; but she knows my mind well enough, and I know hers."

"Then you know more than I do," said the mother, ironically.

He thought over this conversation, and very wisely determined not to run unnecessary risks: he came up one afternoon, and hunted about for Mercy, till he found her milking a cow in the adjoining paddock.

"Well, lass," said he, "I've good news for thee. My old dad says we may have his house to live in. So now you and I can yoke next month if ye will."
"Me turn the honest man out of his house!" said Mercy, mighty innocently.

"Who asks you? He nobbut bargains for the chimney corner: and you are not the girl to begrudge the old man that."

"Oh no, Paul. But what would father do if I were to leave his house? Methinks the farm would go to rack and ruin; he is so wrapped up in his nasty public."

"Why, he has got a helper, by all accounts: and if you talk like that, you will never wed at all."

"Never is a big word. But I'm too young to marry yet. Jenny, thou jade, stand still."

The attack and defence proceeded upon these terms for some time; and the defendant had one base advantage; and used it. Her forehead was wedged tight against Jenny's ribs, and Paul could not see her face. This, and the feminine evasiveness of her replies, irritated him at last.

"Take thy head out o' the coow," said he, roughly, "and answer straight. Is all our wooing to go for nought?"

"Wooing? You never said so much to me in all these years, as you have to-day."

"Oh, ye knew my mind well enough. There's a many ways of showing the heart."

"Speaking out is the best, I trow."

"Why, what do I come here for twice a week, this two years past, if not for thee?"

"Ay, for me, and father's ale."

"And thou canst look at me, and tell me that? Ye false hard-hearted hussy. But, nay, thou wast never so: 'tis this Thomas Leicester hath bewitched thee, and set thee against thy true lover."

"Mr. Leicester pays no suit to me," said Mercy, blushing: "he is a right civil-spoken gentleman, and you know you saved his life."

"The more fool I. I wish I had known he was going to rob me of my lass's heart, I'd have seen him die a hundred times ere I'd have interfered. But they say if you save a man's life he'll make you rue it. Mercy, my lass, you are well respected in the parish; take a thought now: better be a farrier's wife than a gentleman's mistress."

Mercy did take her head "out of the cow" at this, and, for once, her cheek burned with anger; but the unwonted sentiment died before it could find words, and she said, quietly, "I need not be either, against my will."

Young Carrick made many such appeals to Mercy Vint; but he could never bring her to confess to him that he and she had ever been more than friends, or were now anything less than friends. Still he forced her to own to herself, that, if she had never seen Thomas Leicester, her quiet affection and respect for Garrick would probably have carried her to the altar with him.

His remonstrances, sometimes angry, sometimes tearful, awoke her pity, which was the grand sentiment of her heart, and disturbed her peace.

Moreover, she studied the two men in her quiet, thoughtful way, and saw that Carrick loved her with all his honest, though hitherto tepid heart; but Griffith had depths, and could love with more passion than ever he had shown for her. "He is not the man to have a fever by reason of me," said the poor girl, to herself. But I am afraid even this attracted her to Griffith; it nettled a woman's soft ambition; which is, to be as well loved as ever woman was.

And so things went on, and, as generally happens, the man who was losing ground went the very way to lose more. He spoke ill of Griffith behind his back: called him a highwayman, a gentleman, an ungrateful, undermining traitor. But Griffith never mentioned Carrick; and so when he and Mercy were together, her old follower was pleasingly obliterated, and affectionate good humour reigned. Thus Griffith, alias Thomas, became her sunbeam, and Paul her cloud.

But he who had disturbed the peace of others, his own turn came.

One day he found Mercy crying: he sat clown beside her, and said, kindly, "Why, sweetheart, what is amiss?"

"No great matter," said she; and turned her head away, but did not check her tears, for it was new and pleasant to be consoled by Thomas Leicester.

"Nay, but tell me, child."

"Well, then, Jessie Carrick has been at me; that is all."

"The vixen! what did she say?"

"Nay, I'm not pleased enow with it to repeat it. She did cast something in my teeth."

Griffith pressed her to be more explicit: she declined, with so many blushes, that his curiosity was awakened, and he told Mrs. Vint, with some heat, that Jess Carrick had been making Mercy cry.

"Like enow," said Mrs. Vint, coolly. "She'll eat her victuals all one for that, please God."

"Else I'll ring the cock-nosed jade's neck, next time she comes here," replied Griffith; "but, dame, I want to know what she can have to say to Mercy to make her cry."

Mrs. Vint looked him steadily in the face for some time, and then and there decided to come to an explanation. "Ten to one 'tis about her brother," said she; "you know this Paul is our Mercy's sweetheart."

At these simple words Griffith winced, and his countenance changed remarkably. Mrs. Vint observed it, and was all the more resolved to have it out with him.

"Her sweetheart!" said Griffith. "Why, I have seen them together a dozen of times, and not a word of courtship."

"Oh, the young men don't make many speeches in these parts. They show their hearts by act." "By act? why, I met them coming home from milking t' other evening. Mercy was carrying the pail, brimful; and that oaf sauntered by her side, with his hands in his pockets; was that the act of a lover?"

"I heard of it, sir," said Mrs. Vint, quietly; "and as how you took the pail from her, willy nilly, and carried it home. Mercy was vexed about it: she told me you panted at the door, and she was a deal fitter to carry the pail than you, that is just off a sick bed, like. But lawk, sir, ye can't go by the likes of that: the bachelors here they'd see their sweethearts carry the roof into next parish on their backs, like a snail, and never put out a hand; 'tis not the custom hereaway: but, as I was saying, Paul and our Mercy kept company, after a manner: he never had the wit to flatter her as should be, nor the stomach to bid her name, the day, and he'd buy the ring; but he talked to her about his sick beasts more than he did to any other girl in the parish, and she'd have ended by going to church with him; only you came and put a coolness atween 'em."

"I! How?"

"Well, sir, our Mercy is a kind-hearted lass, though I say it, and you were sick, and she did nurse you; and that was a beginning. And, to be sure, you are a fine personable man, and capital company; and you are always about the girl; and, bethink you, sir, she is flesh and blood like her neighbours; and they say, once a body has tasted venison steak, it spoils their stomach for oat porridge. Now that is Mercy's case, I'm thinking; not that she ever said as much to me; she is too reserved. But bless your heart, I'm forced to go about with eyes in my head, and watch 'em all a bit, me that keeps an inn."

Griffith groaned. "I'm a villain!" said he.

"Nay, nay," said Mrs. Vint. "'Gentlefolks must be amused, cost what it may; but, hoping no offence, sir, the girl was a good friend to you in time of sickness; and so was this Paul, for that matter."

"She was," cried Griffith; "God bless her. How can I ever repay her?"

"Well, sir," said Mrs. Vint, "if that comes from your heart, you might take our Mercy apart, and tell her you like her very well, but not enough to marry a farmer's daughter—don't say an inn-keeper's daughter, or you'll be sure to offend her; she is bitter against the 'Packhorse.' Says you, 'This Paul is an honest lad, turn your heart back to him.' And, with that, mount your black horse and ride away, and God speed you, sir; we shall often talk of you at the 'Packhorse,' and nought but good."

Griffith gave the woman his hand, and his breast laboured visibly.

Jealousy was ingrained in the man. Mrs. Vint had pricked his conscience, but she had wounded his foible.

He was not in love with Mercy, but he esteemed her and liked her and saw her value, and, above all, could not bear another man should have her.

Now this gave the matter a new turn. Mrs. Vint had overcome her dislike to him long ago: still he was not her favourite. But his giving her his hand with a gentle pressure, and his manifest agitation, rather won her: and, as uneducated women are your true weathercocks, she went about directly. "To be sure," said she, "our Mercy is too good for the likes of him; she is not like Harry and me: she has been well brought up by her Aunt Prudence, as was governess in a nobleman's house. She can read and write, and cast accounts; good at her sampler, and can churn and make cheeses, and play of the viol, and lead the psalm in church, and dance a minuet, she can, with any lady in the land. As to her nursing in time of sickness, that I leave to you, sir.

"She is an angel," cried Griffith, "and my benefactress: no man living is good enough for her." And he went away, visibly discomposed.

Mrs. Vint repeated this conversation to Mercy, and told her Thomas Leicester was certainly in love with her. "Shouldst have seen his face, girl, when I told him Paul and you were sweethearts. 'Twas as if I had run a knife in his heart."

Mercy murmured a few words of doubt; but she kissed her mother eloquently, and went about rosy and beaming, all that afternoon.

As for Griffith, his gratitude and his jealousy were now at war, and caused him a severe mental struggle.

Carrick, too, was spurred by jealousy, and came every day to the house, and besieged Blercy; and Griffith, who saw them together, and did not hear Mercy's replies, was excited, irritated, alarmed.

Mrs. Vint saw his agitation, and determined to bring matters to a climax. She was always giving him a side thrust; and, at last, she told him plainly that he was not behaving like a man. "If the girl is not good enough for you, why make a fool of her, and set her against a good husband?" And when he replied she was good enough for any man in England, "Then," said she, "why not show your respect for her as Paul Carrick does? He likes her well enough to go to church with her."

With the horns of this dilemma she so gored Kate Peyton's husband that, at last, she and Paul Carrick, between them, drove him out of his conscience.

So he watched his opportunity and got Mercy alone: he took her hand and told her he loved her, and that she was his only comfort in the world, and he found he could not live without her.

At this she blushed and trembled a little, and leaned her brow upon his shoulder, and was a happy creature for a few moments.

So far, fluently enough; but then he began to falter and stammer, and say that for certain reasons, he could not marry at all. But if she could be content with anything short of that, he would retire with her into a distant country, and there, where nobody could contradict him, would call her his wife, and treat her as his wife, and pay his debt of gratitude to her by a life of devotion.

As he spoke, her brow retired an inch or two from his shoulder; but she heard him quietly out, and then drew back and confronted him, pale, but to all appearance, calm.

"Call things by their right names," said she. "What you offer me this day, in my father's house, is, to be your mistress. Then—God forgive you, Thomas Leicester."

With this oblique and feminine reply, and one look of unfathomable reproach from her soft eyes, she turned her back on him; but remembering her manners, curtsied at the door; and so retired; and unpretending Virtue lent her such true dignity, that he was struck dumb, and made no attempt to detain her.

I think her dignified composure did not last long when she was alone; at least, the next time he saw her, her eyes were red; his heart smote him, and he began to make excuses and beg her forgiveness. But she interrupted him. "Don't speak to me no more, if you please, sir," said she, civilly, but coldly.

Mercy, though so quiet and inoffensive, had depth and strength of character. She never told her mother what Thomas Leicester had proposed to her. Her honest pride kept her silent, for one thing. She would not have it known she had been insulted. And, besides that, she loved Thomas Leicester still, and could not expose or hurt him. Once there was an Israelite without guile; though you and I never saw him; and once there was a Saxon without bile; and her name was Mercy Vint. In this heart of gold the affections were stronger than the passions. She was deeply wounded, and showed it in a patient way to him who had wounded her, but to none other. Her conduct to him in public and private was truly singular, and would alone have stamped her a remarkable character. She declined all communication with him in private, and avoided him steadily and adroitly; but in public she spoke to him, sang with him, when she was asked, and treated him much the same as before. He could see a subtle difference, but nobody else could.

This generosity, coupled with all she had done for him before, penetrated his heart and filled him with admiration and remorse. He yielded to Mrs. Vint's suggestions; and told her she was right; he would tear himself away, and never see the dear "Packhorse" again, "But, oh, dame," said he, "'tis a sorrowful thing to be alone in the world again, and nought to do. If I had but a farm, and a sweet little inn like this, perchance my heart would not be quite so heavy as 'tis this day at thoughts of parting from thee and thine."

"Well, sir," said Mrs. Vint, "if that is all, there is the 'Vine' to let at this moment. 'Tis a better place of business than this; and some meadows go with it, and land to be had in the parish."

"I'll ride and see it," said Griffith, eagerly: then, dejectedly, "but, alas, I have no heart to keep an inn without somebody to help me, and say a kind word now and then. Ah, Mercy Vint, thou hast spoiled me for living alone."

This vacillation exhausted Mrs. Vint's patience. "What are ye sighing about, ye foolish man?" said she, contemptuously; "you have got it all your own way: if 'tis a wife ye want, ask Mercy, and don't take a nay: if ye would have a housekeeper, you need not want one long. I'll be bound there's plenty of young women where you came from as would be glad to keep the 'Vine' under you. And, if you come to that, our Mercy is a treasure on the farm, but she is no help in the inn, no more than a wax figure: she never brought us a shilling, till you came and made her sing to your base viol. Nay, what you want is a smart handsome girl, with a quick eye and a ready tongue, and one as can look a man in the face, and not given to love nor liquor. Don't you know never such a one?"

"Not I. Humph, to be sure there is Caroline Ryder. She is handsome, and hath a good wit. She is a lady's maid."

"That's your woman, if she'll come. And to be sure she will; for to be mistress of an inn, that's a lady's maid's Paradise."

"She would have come a few months ago, and gladly: I'll write to her."

"Better talk to her, and persuade her."

"I'll do that too; but I must write to her first."

"So do then; but whatever you do, don't shilly-shally no longer. If wrestling was shilly-shallying, methinks you'd bear the bell, you or else Paul Carrick. Why, all this trouble comes on't. He might have wed our Mercy a year agone for the asking. Shilly-shally belongs to us that be women. 'Tis despisable in a man."

Thus driven on all sides, Griffith rode and inspected the "Vine" (it was only seven miles off): and after the usual chaffering, came to terms with the proprietor.

He fixed the day for his departure, and told Mrs. Vint he must ride into Cumberland first to get some money, and also to see about a housekeeper.

He made no secret of all this; and, indeed, was not without hopes Mercy would relent, or perhaps be jealous of this housekeeper. But the only visible effect was to make her look pale and sad: she avoided him in private as before.

Harry Vint was loud in his regrets, and Carrick openly exultant. Griffith wrote to Caroline Ryder, and addressed the latter in a feigned hand, and took it himself to the nearest post town.

The letter came to hand, and will appear in that sequence of events on which I am now about to enter.

CHAPTER XIII

If Griffith Gaunt suffered anguish, he inflicted agony. Mrs. Gaunt was a high-spirited, proud, and sensitive woman; and he crushed her with foul words. Leonard was a delicate, vain, and sensitive man, accustomed to veneration. Imagine such a man hurled to the ground, and trampled upon.

Griffith should not have fled; he should have stayed and enjoyed his vengeance on these two persons. It might have cooled him a little had he stopped and seen the immediate consequences of his savage act.

The priest rose from the ground, pale as ashes, and trembling with fear and hate.

The lady was leaning, white as a sheet, against a tree, and holding it with her very nails for a little support.

They looked round at one another; a piteous glance of anguish and horror: then Mrs. Gaunt turned and flung her arm round so that the palm of her hand, high raised, confronted Leonard. I am thus particular, because it was a gesture grand and terrible as the occasion that called it forth: a gesture that spoke; and said, "Put the whole earth and sea between us for ever after this."

The next moment she bent her head and rushed away, cowering and wringing her hands: she made for her house as naturally as a scared animal for its lair; but, ere she could reach it, she tottered under the shame, the distress, and the mere terror, and fell fainting with her fair forehead on the grass.

Caroline Ryder was crouched in the doorway, and did not see her come out of the grove, but only heard a rustle, and then saw her proud mistress totter forward and lie white, senseless, helpless at her very feet.

Ryder littered a scream, but did not lose her presence of mind. She instantly kneeled over Mrs. Gaunt, and loosened her stays with quick and dexterous hand.

It was very like the hawk perched over and clawing the ringdove she has struck down.

But people with brains are never quite inhuman: a drop of lukewarm pity entered even Ryder's heart as she assisted her victim. She called no one to help her; for she saw something very serious had happened, and she felt sure Mrs. Gaunt would say something imprudent in that dangerous period when the patient recovers consciousness but has not all her wits about her. Now Ryder was equally determined to know her mistress's secrets, and not to share the knowledge with any other person.

It was a long swoon; and, when Mrs. Gaunt came to, the first thing she saw was Ryder leaning over her, with a face of much curiosity, and some concern.

In that moment of weakness the poor lady, who had keen so roughly handled, saw a woman close to her, and being a little kind to her; so what did she do but throw her arms round Ryder's neck and burst out sobbing as if her heart would break.

Then that unprincipled woman shed a tear or two with her, half-crocodile, half impulse.

Mrs. Gaunt not only cried on her servant's neck; she justified Ryder's forecast by speaking unguardedly: "I've been insulted—insulted—insulted!"

But, even while uttering these words, she was recovering her pride: so the first "insulted" seemed to come from a broken-hearted child, the second from an indignant lady the third from a wounded queen.

No more words than this; but rose, with Ryder's assistance, and went, leaning on that faithful creature's shoulder, to her own bedroom. There she sank into a chair, and said, in a voice to melt a stone, "My child! Bring me my little Rose."

Ryder ran and fetched the little girl and Mrs. Gaunt held out both arms to her, angelically, and clasped her so passionately and piteously to her bosom, that Rose cried for fear, and never forgot the scene all her days: and Mrs. Ryder, who was secretly a mother, felt a genuine twinge of pity and remorse. Curiosity, however, was the dominant sentiment: she was impatient to get all these convulsions over, and learn what had actually passed between Mr. and Mrs. Gaunt.

She waited till her mistress appeared calmer: and then, in soft caressing tones, asked her what had happened.

"Never ask me that question again," cried Mrs. Gaunt, wildly: then, with inexpressible dignity, "my good girl, you have done all you could for me; now you must leave me alone with my daughter, and my God, who knows the truth."

Ryder curtsied and retired, burning with baffled curiosity.

Towards dusk Thomas Leicester came into the kitchen, and brought her news with a vengeance. He told her and the other maids that the Squire had gone raving mad, and fled the country. "Oh, lasses," said he, "if you had seen the poor soul's face, a riding headlong through the fair all one as if it was a ploughed field; 'twas white as your smocks: and his eyes glowering on t'other world. We shall ne'er see that face alive again."

And this was her doing.

It surprised and overpowered Ryder; she threw her apron over her head, and went off in hysterics, and betrayed her lawless attachment to every woman in the kitchen, she who was so clever at probing others.

This day of violent emotions was followed by a sullen and sorrowful gloom.

Mrs. Gaunt kept her bedroom, and admitted nobody; till, at last, the servants consulted together, and sent little Rose to knock at her door, with a basin of chocolate, while they watched on the stairs.

"It's only me, mamma," said Rose.

"Come in, my precious," said a trembling voice, and so Rose got in with her chocolate.

The next day she was sent for early: and at noon, Mrs. Gaunt and Rose came downstairs; but their appearance startled the whole household.

The mother was dressed all in black, and so was her daughter, whom she led by the hand. Mrs. Gaunt's face was pale, and sad, and stem; a monument of deep suffering, and high-strung resolution.

It soon transpired that Griffith had left his home for good: and friends called on Mrs. Gaunt to slake their curiosity under the mask of sympathy.

Not one of them was admitted. No false excuses were made. "My mistress sees no one for the present," was the reply.

Curiosity, thus baffled, took up the pen; but was met with a short unvarying formula: "There is an unhappy misunderstanding between my husband and me. But I shall neither accuse him behind his back, nor justify myself."

Thus the proud lady carried herself before the world; but secretly she writhed. A wife abandoned is a woman insulted, and makes the wives, that are not abandoned—cluck.

Ryder was dejected for a time, and, though not honestly penitent, suffered some remorse at the miserable issue of her intrigues. But her elastic nature soon shook it off, and she felt a certain satisfaction at having reduced Mrs. Gaunt to her own level. This disarmed, her hostility: she watched her as keenly as ever, but out of pure curiosity.

One thing puzzled her strangely. Leonard did not visit the house; nor could she even detect any communication between the parties.

At last, one day, her mistress told her to put on her hat and go to Father Leonard.

Ryder's eyes sparkled; and she was soon equipped. Mrs. Gaunt put a parcel and a letter into her hands. Ryder no sooner got out of her sight than she proceeded to tamper with the letter. But to her just indignation she found it so ingeniously folded and sealed that she could not read a word.

The parcel, however, she easily undid, and it contained forty pounds in gold and small notes. "Oho! my lady," said Ryder.

She was received by Leonard with a tender emotion he in vain tried to conceal.

On reading the letter his features contracted sharply, and he seemed to suffer agony. He would not even open the parcel. "You will take that hack," said he, bitterly.

"What, without a word?"

"Without a word. But I will write, when I am able."

"Don't be long, sir," suggested Ryder. "I am sure my mistress is wearying for you. Consider, sir, she is all alone now."

"Not so much alone as I am," said the priest: "nor half so unfortunate."

And with this he leaned his head despairingly on his hand, and motioned to Ryder to leave him.

"Here's a couple of fools," said she to herself, as she went home.

That very evening Thomas Leicester caught her alone, and asked her to marry him.

She stared at first, and then treated it as a jest.

"You come at the wrong time, young man," said she. "Marriage is put out of countenance. No, no, I will never marry, after what I have seen in this house."

Leicester would not take this for an answer, and pressed her hard.

"Thomas," said this plausible jade, "I like you very well; but I couldn't leave my mistress in her trouble. Time to talk of marrying when master comes here alive and well."

"Nay," said Leicester, "my only chance is while he is away: you care more for his little finger than for my whole body; that they all say."

"Who says?"

"Jane, and all the lasses."

"You simple man, they want you for themselves; that is why they belie me."

"Nay, nay; I saw how you carried on, when I brought word he was gone. You let your heart out for once. Don't take me for a fool: I see how 'tis: but I'll face it: for I worship the ground you walk on. Take a thought, my lass. What good can come of your setting your heart on him? I'm young, I'm healthy, and not ugly enough to set the dogs a barking: I've got a good place; I love you dear; I'll cure you of that fancy, and make you as happy as the day is long. I'll try and make you as happy as you will make me, my beauty."

He was so earnest, and so much in love, that Mrs. Ryder pitied him, and wished her husband was in Heaven.

"I am very sorry, Tom," said she, softly: "dear me, I did not think you cared so much for me as this. I must just tell you the truth. I have got one in my own country, and I've promised him. I don't care to break my word: and, if I did, he is such a man, I am sure he would kill me for it. Indeed he has told me as much, more than once or twice."

"Killing is a game that two can play at."

"Ah! but 'tis an ugly game: and I'll have no hand in it. And—don't you be angry with me, Tom—I've known him longest, and—I love him best."

By pertinacity and variety in lying, she hit the mark at last. Tom swallowed this figment whole.

"That is but reason," said he. "I take my answer, and I wish ye both many happy days together, and well spent."

With this he retired, and blubbered a good hour in an outhouse.

Tom avoided the castle, and fell into low spirits. He told his mother all, and she advised him to change the air. "You have been too long in one place," said she; "I hate being too long in one place myself."

This fired Tom's gipsy blood, and he said he would travel to-morrow, if he could but scrape together money enough to fill a pedlar's pack.

He applied for a loan in several quarters, but was denied in all.

At last the poor fellow summoned courage to lay his case before Mrs. Gaunt.

Ryder's influence procured him an interview. She took him into the drawing-room, and bade him wait there. By and by a pale lady, all in black, glided into the room.

He pulled his front hair, and began to stammer something or other.

She interrupted him. "Ryder has told me," said she, softly. "I am sorry for you: and I will do what you require. And, to be sure, we need no gamekeeper here now."

She then gave him some money, and said she would look him up a few trifles besides, to put in his pack.

Toni's mother helped him to lay out this money to advantage, and one day he called at Hernshaw, pack and all, to bid farewell.

The servants all laid out something with him for luck: and Mrs. Gaunt sent for him, and gave him a gold thimble, and a pound of tea, and several yards of gold lace, slightly tarnished, and a Queen Anne's guinea.

He thanked her heartily. "Ay, Dame," said he, "you had always an open hand, married or single. My heart is heavy at leaving you. But I miss the Squire's kindly face too. Hernshaw is not what it used to be."

Mrs. Gaunt turned her head aside, and the man could see his words had made her cry.

"My good Thomas," said she, at last, "you are going to travel the country: you might fall in with him."

"I might," said Leicester, incredulously.

"God grant you may: and, if ever you should, think of your poor mistress, and give him—this." She put her finger into her bosom and drew out a bullet wrapped in silver paper. "You will never lose this," said she. "I value it more than gold or silver. Oh, if ever you *should* see him, think of me and my daughter, and just put it in his hand without a word."

As he went out of the room Ryder intercepted him, and said, "Mayhap you will fall in with our master: if ever you do, tell him he is under a mistake, and the sooner he comes home the better." Tom Leicester departed: and, for days and weeks, nothing occurred to break the sorrowful monotony of the place.

But the mourner had written to her old friend and confessor Francis: and, after some delay, involuntary on his part, he came to see her.

They were often closeted together, and spoke so low that Ryder could not catch a word.

Francis also paid several visits to Leonard; and the final result of these visits was that the latter left England.

Francis remained at Hernshaw as long as he could; and it was Mrs. Gaunt's hourly prayer that Griffith might return while Francis was with her.

Ho did, at her earnest request, stay much longer than he had intended; but, at length, he was obliged to fix next Monday to return to his own place.

It was on Thursday he made this arrangement; but the very next day the postman brought a letter to the Castle, thus addressed:—

"To Mistress Caroline Ryder,

"Living Servant with Griffith Gaunt, Esq.,

"at his house, called Hernshaw Castle,

"near Wigeonmoor,

"in the county of Cumberland.

"These with speed."

The address was in a feigned hand. Ryder opened it in the kitchen, and uttered a scream.

Instantly three female throats opened upon her with questions.

She looked them contemptously in them faces, put the letter into her pocket; and, soon after, slipped away to her own room, and locked herself in while she read it. It ran thus:——

> "GOOD MISTRESS RYDER,—I am alive yet, by the blessing; though somewhat battered; being now risen from a fever, wherein I lost my wits for a time. And, on coming to myself,

I found them making of my shroud; whereby you shall learn how near I was to death. And all this I owe to that false perjured woman that was my wife, and is your mistress.

"Know that I have donned russet and doffed gentility; for I find a heavy heart's best cure is occupation. I have taken a wayside inn, and think of renting a small farm, which two things go well together. Now you are, of all those I know, most fitted to manage the inn, and I the farm. You were always my good friend: and, if you be so still, then I charge you most solemnly that you utter no word to any living soul about this letter; but meet me privately where we can talk fully of these matters; for I will not set foot in Hernshaw Castle. Moreover, she told me once 'twas hers; and so be it. On Friday I shall be at Stapleton, and the next day, by an easy journey, to the place where I once was so happy.

"So then at seven of the clock on Saturday evening, be the same wet or dry, prithee come to the gate of the Grove unbeknown, and speak to

"Your faithful friend

"and most unhappy master,

"GRIFFITH GAUNT.

"Be secret as the grave. Would I were in it."

This letter set Caroline Ryder in a tumult. Griffith alive and well, and set against his wife, and coming to her for assistance!

After the first agitation she read it again, and weighed every syllable. There was one book she had studied more than most of us—the Heart. And she soon read Griffith's in this letter. It was no love-letter: he really intended business: but, weak in health, and broken in spirit, and alone in the world, he naturally turned to one who had confessed an affection for him, and would therefore be true to his interests, and study his happiness.

The proposal was every way satisfactory to Mrs. Ryder. To be mistress of an inn, and have servants under her instead of being one herself. And then, if Griffith and she began as allies in business, she felt very sure she could make herself, first necessary to him, and then dear to him.

She was so elated she could hardly contain herself; and all her fellow servants remarked that Mrs. Ryder had heard good news.

Saturday came, and never did hours seem to creep so slowly.

But at last the sun set, and the stars came out: there was no moon. Ryder opened the window and looked out: it was an admirable night for an assignation.

She washed her face again, put on her grey silk gown, and purple petticoat—Mrs. Gaunt had given them to her—and, at the last moment, went and made up her mistress's fire, and put out everything she thought could be wanted, and, five minutes after seven o'clock, tied a scarlet handkerchief over her head, and stepped out at the back door.

What with her coal black hair, so streaked with red, her black eyes, flashing in the starlight, and her glowing cheeks, she looked bewitching.

And, thus armed for conquest, wily, yet impassioned, she stole out, with noiseless foot and beating heart, to her appointment with her imprudent master.

CHAPTER XIV

The bill was paid; the black horse saddled and brought round to the door. Mr. and Mrs. Vint stood bareheaded to honour the parting guest; and the latter offered him the stirrup cup.

Griffith looked round for Mercy; she was nowhere to be seen.

Then he said, piteously, to Mrs. Vint, "What, not even bid me good-bye?"

Mrs. Vint replied, in a very low voice, that there was no disrespect intended. "The truth is, sir, she could not trust herself to see you go; but she bade me give you a message. Says she, 'Mother, tell him I pray God to bless him, go where he will.'"

Something rose in Griffith's throat. "Oh, dame!" said he, "if she only knew the truth, she would think better of me than she does. God bless her!"

And he rode sorrowfully away, alone in the world once more.

At the first turn in the road, he wheeled his horse, and took a last lingering look.

There was nothing vulgar, nor inn-like, in the "Packhorse." It stood fifty yards from the road on a little rural green, and was picturesque itself. The front was entirely clad with large-leaved ivy. Shutters there were none: the windows, with their diamond panes, were lustrous squares, set like great eyes in the green ivy. It looked a pretty, peaceful retreat, and in it Griffith had found peace, and a dove-like friend.

He sighed, and rode away from the sight; not raging and convulsed, as when he rode from Hernshaw Castle, but somewhat sick at heart and very heavy.

He paced so slowly that it took him a quarter of an hour to reach the "Woodman," a wayside inn not two miles distant. As he went by, a farmer hailed him from the porch, and insisted on drinking with him; for he was very popular in the neighbourhood. Whilst they were thus employed, who should come out but Paul Carrick, booted and spurred; and flushed in the face, and rather the worse for liquor imbibed on the spot.

"So you are going, are ye?" said he. "A good job too." Then, turning to the other, "Master Gutteridge, never you save a man's life if you can anywise help it. I saved this one's: and what does he do but turn round and poison my sweetheart against me."

"How can you say so?" remonstrated Griffith. "I never belied you. Your name scarce ever passed my lips."

"Don't tell me," said Carrick. "However, she has come to her senses, and given your worship the sack. Ride you into Cumberland, and I to the 'Packhorse,' and take my own again."

With this he unhooked his nag from the wall, and clattered off to the "Packhorse."

Griffith sat a moment stupified, and then his face was convulsed by his ruling passion. He wheeled his horse, gave him the spur, and galloped after Carrick.

He soon came up with him, and yelled in his ear, "I'll teach you to spit your wormwood in my cup of sorrow."

Carrick shook his fist defiantly, and spurred his horse in turn.

It was an exciting race, and a novel one; but soon decided. The great black hunter went ahead, and still improved his advantage. Carrick, purple with rage, was full a quarter of a mile behind, when Griffith dashed furiously into the stable of the "Packhorse," and, leaving Black Dick panting and covered with foam, ran in search of Mercy.

The girl told him she was in the dairy: he looked in at the window, and there she was with her mother. With instinctive sense and fortitude she had fled to work. She was trying to churn; but it would not do: she had laid her shapely arm all across the churn, and her head on it, and was crying. Mrs. Vint was praising Carrick, and offering homely consolation.

"Ah, mother," sighed Mercy, "I could have made him happy. He does not know that; and he has turned his back on content. What will become of him now?"

Griffith heard no more: he went round to the front door, and rushed in.

"Take your own way, Dame," said he, in great agitation. "Put up the banns when you like. Sweetheart, wilt wed with me? I'll make thee the best husband I can."

Mercy screamed faintly, and lifted up her hands; then she blushed and trembled to her very finger ends; but it ended in smiles of joy and her brow upon his shoulder. In which attitude, with Mrs. Vint patting him approvingly on the back, they were surprised by Paul Carrick. He came to the door, and there stood aghast.

The young man stared ruefully at the picture, and then said, very drily, "I'm too late, methinks."

"That you be, Paul," said Mrs. Vint, cheerfully. "She is meat for your master."

"Don't—you—never—come to me—to save your life—no more," blubbered Paul, breaking down all of a sudden.

He then retired, little heeded, and came no more to the "Packhorse" for several days.

CHAPTER XV

It is desirable that improper marriages should never be solemnized: and the Christian Church saw this many hundred years ago, and ordained that before a marriage, the banns should be cried in a church three Sundays, and any person there present might forbid the union of the parties, and allege the just impediment.

This precaution was feeble, but not wholly inadequate—in the middle ages; for we know by good evidence that the priest was often interrupted and the banns forbidden.

But in modern days the banns are never forbidden: in other words, the precautionary measure that has come down to us from the thirteenth century is out of date and useless. It rests, indeed, on an estimate of publicity, that has become childish. If persons about to marry were compelled to inscribe their names and descriptions in a Matrimonial Weekly Gazette, and a copy of this were placed on a desk in ten thousand churches, perhaps we might stop one lady per annum from marrying her husband's brother, and one gentleman from wedding his neighbour's wife. But the crying of banns in a single parish church is a waste of the people's time and the parson's breath.

And so it proved in Griffith Gaunt's case. The Rev. William Wentworth published, in the usual recitative, the banns of marriage between Thomas Leicester, of the parish of Marylebone in London, and Mercy Vint, spinster, of this parish: and creation, present ex hypothesi mediævale, but absent in fact, assented, by silence, to the union.

So Thomas Leicester wedded Mercy Vint, and took her home to the "Packhorse."

It would be well if those who stifle their consciences, and commit crimes, would set up a sort of medico-moral diary, and record their symptoms minutely day by day. Such records might help to clear away some vague, conventional notions.

To tell the truth, our hero, and now malefactor (the combination is of high antiquity), enjoyed, for several months, the peace of mind that belongs of right to innocence; and his days passed in a state of smooth complacency. Mercy was a good, wise, and tender wife; she naturally looked up to him after marriage more than she did before: she studied his happiness, as she had never studied her own: she mastered his character, admired his good qualities, discerned his weaknesses, but did not view them as defects; only as little traits to be watched, lest she should give pain to "her master," as she called him.

Affection, in her, took a more obsequious form than it could ever assume in Kate Peyton. And yet she had great influence, and softly governed "her master" for his good. She would come into the room and take away the bottle, if he was committing excess; but she had a way of doing it, so like a good but resolute mother, and so unlike a termagant, that he never resisted. Upon the whole, she nursed his mind as, in earlier days, she had nursed his body.

And then she made him so comfortable; she observed him minutely to that end. As is the eye of a maid to the hand of her mistress, so Mercy Leicester's dove-like eye was ever watching "her master's" face, to learn the minutest features of his mind.

One evening he came in tired, and there was a black fire in the parlour. His countenance fell the sixteenth of an inch. You and I, sir, should never have noticed it. But Mercy did, and, ever after, there was a clear fire when he came in.

She noted, too, that he loved to play the viol da gambo; but disliked the trouble of tuning it. So then she tuned it for him.

When he came home at night, early or late, he was sure to find a dry pair of shoes on the rug, his six-stringed viol tuned to a hair, a bright fire, and a brighter wife smiling and radiant at his coming, and always neat: for, said she, "Shall I don my bravery for strangers, and not for my Thomas, that is the best of company?"

They used to go to church, and come back together, hand in hand like lovers: for the arm was rarely given in those days. And Griffith said to himself every Sunday, "What a comfort to have a Protestant wife."

But one day he was off his guard, and called her "Kate, my dear."

"Who is Kate?" said she, softly; but with a degree of trouble and intelligence that made him tremble.

"No matter," said he, all in a flutter: then, solemnly, "Whoever she was, she is dead; dead."

"Ah!" said Mercy, very tenderly and solemnly, and under her breath. "You loved her; yet she must die." She paused; then, in a tone so exquisite I can only call it an angel's whisper, "Poor Kate!"

Griffith groaned aloud. "For God's sake never mention that name to me again. Let me forget she ever lived. She was not the true friend to me that you have been."

Mercy replied, softly, "Say not so, Thomas. You loved her well. Her death had all but cost me thine. Ah, well! we cannot all be the first. I am not very jealous, for my part; and I thank God for't. Thou art a dear good husband to me, and that is enow."

Paul Carrick, unable to break off his habits, came to the "Packhorse" now and then; but Mercy protected her husband's heart from pain. She was kind, and even pitiful; but so discreet and resolute, and contrived to draw the line so clearly between her husband and her old sweetheart, that Griffith's foible could not burn him, for want of fuel.

And so passed several months, and the man's heart was at peace. He could not love Mercy passionately as he had loved Kate; but he was full of real regard and esteem for her: it was one of those gentle, clinging attachments that outlast grand passions, and survive till death; a tender, pure affection; though built upon a crime.

They had been married, and lived in sweet content, about three quarters of a year—when trouble came; but in a vulgar form. A murrain carried off several of Harry Vint's cattle; and it then came out that he had purchased six of them on credit, and had been induced to set his hands to bills of exchange for them. His rent was also behind, and, in fact, his affairs were in a desperate condition.

He hid it as long as he could from them all; but, at last, being served with a process for debt, and threatened with a distress, and an execution, he called a family council and exposed the real state of things.

Mrs. Vint rated him soundly for keeping all this secret so long.

He whom they called Thomas Leicester remonstrated with him. "Had you told me in time," said he, "I had not paid forfeit for 'The Vine,' but settled there, and given you a home."

Mercy said never a word but "Poor father!"

As the peril drew nearer, the conversation became more animated and agitated, and soon the old people took to complaining of Thomas Leicester to his wife.

"Thou hast married a gentleman; and he hath not the heart to lift a hand to save thy folk from ruin."

"Say not so," pleaded Mercy: "to be sure he hath the heart, but not the means. 'Twas but yestreen he bade me sell his jewels for you. But, mother, I think they belonged to some one he loved; and she died. So, poor thing, how could I? Then, if you love me, blame me, and not him."

"Jewels, quotha! will they stop such a gap as ours?" was the contemptuous reply.

From complaining of him behind his back, the old people soon came to launching innuendoes obliquely at him. Here is one specimen out of a dozen.

"Wife, if our Mercy had wedded one of her own sort, mayhap he'd have helped us a bit."

"Ay, poor soul; and she so near her time: if the bailiffs come down on us next month 'tis my belief we shall lose her as well as house and home."

The false Thomas Leicester let them run on, in dogged silence; but every word was a stab.

And, one day, when he had been baited sore with hints, he turned round on them fiercely, and said, "Did I get you into this mess? It's all your own doing. Learn to see your own faults, and not be so hard on one that has been the best servant you ever had, gentleman or not."

Men can resist the remonstrances that wound them, and so irritate them, better than they can those gentle appeals that rouse no anger, but soften the whole heart. The old people stung him; but Mercy, without design, took a surer way. She never said a word; but sometimes, when the discussions were at their height, she turned her dove-like eyes on him, with a look so loving, so humbly inquiring, so timidly imploring, that his heart melted within him.

Ah, that is a true touch of nature, and genuine observation of the sexes, in the old song—

> My feyther urged me sair;
> My mither didna speak;
> But she looked me in the face,
> Till my hairt was like to break.

These silent, womanly, imploring looks of patient Mercy, were mightier than argument, or invective.

The man knew all along where to get money, and how to get it. He had only to go to Hernshaw Castle. But his very soul shuddered at the idea. However, for Mercy's sake, he took the first step: he compelled himself to look the thing in the face, and discuss it with himself. A few months ago he could not have done this, he loved his lawful wife too much; hated her too much. But now, Mercy, and Time, had blunted both those passions; and he could ask himself whether he could not encounter Kate and her priest without any very violent emotion.

When they first set up house together, he had spent his whole fortune, a sum of two thousand pounds, on repairing and embellishing Hernshaw Castle and grounds. Since she had driven him out of the house, he had a clear right to have back the money; and now he resolved he would have it; only what he wanted was to get it without going to the place in person.

And now Mercy's figure, as well as her imploring looks, moved him greatly. She was in that condition which appeals to a man's humanity, and masculine pity, as well as to his affection. To use the homely words of Scripture, she was great with child: and, in that condition, moved slowly about him, filling his pipe, and laying his slippers, and ministering to all his little comforts; she would make no difference: and when he saw the poor dove move about him so heavily, and rather languidly, yet so zealously and tenderly, the man's very bowels yearned over her, and he felt as if he could die to do her a service.

So, one day, when she was standing by him, bending over his little round table, and filling his pipe with her neat hand, he took her by the other hand and drew her gently on his knee, her burden and all.

"Child!" said he, "do not thou fret. I know how to get money; and I'll do't, for thy sake."

"I know that," said she, softly; "can I no read thy face by this time?" and so laid her cheek to his. "But, Thomas, for my sake, get it honestly; or not at all," said she, still filling his pipe, with her cheek to his, "I'll but take back my own," said he; "fear nought."

But, after thus positively pledging himself to Mercy, he became thoughtful and rather fretful; for he was still most averse to go to Hernshaw, and yet could hit upon no other way; since to employ an agent would be to let out that he had committed bigamy; and so risk his own neck, and break Mercy's heart.

After all his scale was turned by his foible.

Mrs. Vint had been weak enough to confide her trouble to a friend: it was all over the parish in three days.

Well, one day, in the kitchen of the inn, Paul Carrick having drunk two pints of good ale, said to Vint, "Landlord, you ought to have married her to me. I've got two hundred pounds laid by. I'd have pulled you out of the mire, and welcome."

"Would you, though, Paul?" said Harry Vint; "then, by G— —, I wish I had."

Now Carrick bawled that out, and Griffith, who was at the door, heard it.

He walked into the kitchen, ghastly pale, and spoke to Harry Vint first.

"I take your inn, your farm, and your debts, on me," said he; "not one without t'other."

"Spoke like a man!" cried the landlord, joyfully: "and so be it—before these witnesses."

Griffith turned on Carrick: "This house is mine. Get out on't, ye jealous, mischief-making cur." And he took him by the collar and dragged him furiously out of the place, and sent him whirling into the middle of the road; then ran back for his hat and flung it out after him.

This done, he sat down boiling, and his eyes roved fiercely round the room in search of some other antagonist. But his strength was so great, and his face so altered with this sudden spasm of reviving jealousy, that nobody cared to provoke him farther.

After a while, however, Harry Vint muttered, drily, "There goes one good customer."

Griffith took him up sternly: "If your debts are to be mine, your trade shall be mine too, that you had not the head to conduct."

"So be it, son-in-law," said the old man; "only you go so fast: you do take possession afore you pays the fee."

Griffith winced. "That shall be the last of your taunts, old man." He turned to the ostler, "Bill, give Black Dick his oats at sunrise: and in ten days at farthest I'll pay every shilling this house and farm do owe. Now, Master White, you'll put in hand a new sign-board for this inn; a fresh 'Packhorse,' and paint him jet black, with one white hoof (instead of chocolate), in honour of my nag Dick; and in place of Harry Vint you'll put in Thomas Leicester. See that is done against I come back, or come you here no more." Soon after this scene he retired to tell Mercy: and on his departure, the suppressed tongues went like mill-clacks.

Dick came round saddled at peep of day; but Mercy had been up more than an hour, and prepared her man's breakfast. She clung to him at parting, and cried a little; and whispered something in his ear, for nobody else to hear: it was an entreaty that he would not be long gone, lest he should be far from her in the hour of her peril.

Thereupon he promised her, and kissed her tenderly, and bade her be of good heart; and so rode away northwards with dogged resolution.

As soon as he was gone, Mercy's tears flowed without restraint.

Her father set himself to console her. "Thy good man," he said, "is but gone back to the high road for a night or two, to follow his trade of 'stand and deliver.' Fear nought, child; his pistols are well primed; I saw to that myself; and his horse is the fleetest in the county; you'll have him back in three days, and money in both pockets. I warrant you his is a better trade than mine; and he is a fool to change it."

Griffith was two days upon the road, and all that time he was turning over and discussing in his mind how he should conduct the disagreeable but necessary business he had undertaken.

He determined, at last, to make the visit one of business only: no heat; no reproaches. That lovely, hateful woman might continue to dishonour his name, for he had himself abandoned it. He would not deign to receive any money that was hers; but his own two thousand pounds he would have: and two or three hundred on the spot by way of instalment. And, with these hard views, he drew near to Hernshaw; but the nearer he got, the slower he went; for, what at a distance had seemed tolerably easy, began to get more and more difficult, and repulsive. Moreover, his heart, which he thought he had steeled, began now to flutter a little, and somehow to shudder at the approaching interview.

CHAPTER XVI

Caroline Ryder went to the gate of the Grove, and stayed there two hours; but, of course, no Griffith came.

She returned the next night, and the next: and then she gave it up, and awaited an explanation. None came, and she was bitterly disappointed, and indignant.

She began to hate Griffith, and to conceive a certain respect, and even a tepid friendship, for the other woman he had insulted.

Another clue to this change of feeling is to be found in a word she let drop in talking to another servant. "Sly mistress," said she, "bears it like a man."

In fact, Mrs. Gaunt's conduct at this period was truly noble.

She suffered months of torture, months of grief; but the high-spirited creature hid it from the world, and maintained a sad but high composure.

She wore her black, for she said, "How do I know he is alive?" She retrenched her establishment, reduced her expenses two-thirds; and busied herself in works of charity and religion.

Her desolate condition attracted a gentleman who had once loved her, and now esteemed and pitied her profoundly: Sir George Neville.

He was still unmarried, and she was the cause; so far at least as this: she had put him out of conceit with the other ladies at that period when he had serious thoughts of marriage: and the inclination to marry at all had not since returned.

If the Gaunts had settled at Bolton, Sir George would have been their near neighbour; but Neville's Court was nine miles from Hernshaw Castle: and when they met, which was not very often, Mrs. Gaunt was on her guard to give Griffith no shadow of uneasiness. She was therefore rather more dignified and distant with Sir George, than her own inclination and his merits would have prompted; for he was a superior and very agreeable man.

When it became quite certain that her husband had left her, Sir George rode up to Hernshaw Castle, and called upon her.

She begged to be excused from seeing him.

Now, Sir George was universally courted, and this rather nettled him: however, he soon learned that she received nobody except a few religious friends of her own sex.

Sir George then wrote her a letter that did him credit; it was full of worthy sentiment and good sense. For instance, he said he desired to intrude his friendly offices and his sympathy upon her, but nothing more. Time had cured him of those warmer feelings which had once ruffled his peace; but Time could not efface his tender esteem for the lady he had loved in his youth, nor his profound respect for her character.

Mrs. Gaunt wept over his gentle letter, and was on the verge of asking herself why she had chosen Griffith instead of this chevalier. She sent him a sweet, yet prudent reply; she did not encourage him to visit her; but said, that, if ever she should bring herself to receive visits from the gentlemen of the county during her husband's absence, he should be the first to know it. She signed herself his unhappy, but deeply grateful, servant and friend.

One day, as she came out of a poor woman's cottage, with a little basket on her arm, which she had emptied in the cottage, she met Sir George Neville full.

He took his hat off, and made her a profound bow. He was then about to ride on, but altered his mind, and dismounted to speak to her.

The interview was constrained at first; but ere long he ventured to tell her she really ought to consult with some old friend and practical man like himself. He would undertake to scour the country, and find her husband, if he was above ground.

"Me go a hunting the man," cried she, turning red; "not if he was my king as well as my husband. He knows where to find me; and that is enough."

"Well, but madam, would you not like to learn where he is, and what he is doing?"

"Why, yes, my good, kind friend, I should like to know that." And having pronounced these words with apparent calmness, she burst out crying, and almost ran away from him.

Sir George looked sadly after her; and formed a worthy resolution. He saw there was but one road to her regard. He resolved to hunt her husband for her, without intruding on her, or giving her a voice in the matter. Sir George was a magistrate, and accustomed to organize inquiries. Spite of the length of time that had elapsed, he traced Griffith for a considerable distance; pending further inquiries, he sent Mrs. Gaunt word that the truant had not made for the sea, but had gone due south.

Mrs. Gaunt returned him her warm thanks for this scrap of information. So long as Griffith remained in the island there was always a hope he might return to her. The money he had taken would soon be exhausted: and poverty might drive him to her; and she was so far humbled by grief, that she could welcome him even on those terms.

Affliction tempers the proud. Mrs. Gaunt was deeply injured as well as insulted; but, for all that, in her many days and weeks of solitude and sorrow, she took herself to task, and saw her fault. She became more gentle, more considerate of her servants' feelings, more womanly.

For many months she could not enter "the Grove." The spirited woman's very flesh revolted at the sight of the place where she had been insulted and abandoned. But as she went deeper in religion, she forced herself to go to the gate and look in, and say out loud, "I gave the first offence," and then she would go in-doors again, quivering with the internal conflict.

Finally, being a Catholic, and therefore attaching more value to self-torture than we do, the poor soul made this very grove her place of penance Once a week she had the fortitude to drag herself to the very spot where Griffith had denounced her; and there she would kneel and pray for him and for herself. And, certainly, if humility and self-abasement were qualities of the body, here was to be seen their picture; for her way was to set her crucifix up at the foot of a tree; then to bow herself all down, between kneeling and lying; and put her lips meekly to the foot of the crucifix and so pray long and earnestly.

Now, one day, while she was thus crouching in prayer, a gentleman, booted, and spurred, and splashed, drew near, with hesitating steps. She was so absorbed, she did not hear those steps at all, till they were very near; but then she trembled all over; for her delicate ear recognized a manly tread she had not heard for many a day. She dared not move nor look, for she thought it was a mere sound, sent to her by heaven to comfort her.

But the next moment a well-known mellow voice came like a thunder-clap, it shook her so.

"Forgive me, my good dame, but I desire to know——"

The question went no farther, for Kate Gaunt sprang to her feet, with a loud scream, and stood glaring at Griffith Gaunt, and he at her.

And thus husband and wife met again—met, by some strange caprice of Destiny, on the very spot where they had parted so horribly.

CHAPTER XVII

The gaze these two persons bent on one another may be half imagined; it can never be described.

Griffith spoke first. "In black!" said he, in a whisper.

His voice was low; his face, though pale and grim, had not the terrible aspect he wore at parting.

So she thought he had come back in an amicable spirit; and she flew to him with a cry of love, and threw her arm round his neck, and panted on his shoulder.

At this reception, and the tremulous contact of one he had loved so dearly, a strange shudder ran through his frame: a shudder that marked his present repugnance, yet indicated her latent power.

He himself felt he had betrayed some weakness; and it was all the worse for her: he caught her wrist and put her from him, not roughly, but with a look of horror. "The day is gone by for that, madam," he gasped. Then, sternly: "Think you I came here to play the credulous husband?"

Mrs. Gaunt drew back in her turn, and faltered out, "What! come back here, and not sorry for what you have done? not the least sorry? Oh, my heart! you have almost broken it."

"Prithee, no more of this," said Griffith, sternly. "You and I are nought to one another now, and for ever. But there, you are but a woman, and I did not come to quarrel with you." And he fixed his eyes on the ground.

"Thank God for that," faltered Mrs. Gaunt. "Oh, sir, the sight of you—the thought of what you were to me once—till jealousy blinded you. Lend me your arm, if you are a man; my limbs do fail me."

The shock had been too much; a pallor over-spread her lovely features, her knees knocked together, and she was tottering like some tender tree cut down, when Griffith, who, with all his faults, was a man, put out his strong arm, and she clung to it, quivering all over, and weeping hysterically.

That little hand, with its little feminine clutch, trembling on his arm, raised a certain male compassion for her piteous condition; and he bestowed a few cold, sad, words of encouragement on her. "Come, come," said he, gently; "I shall not trouble you long. I'm cured of my jealousy. 'Tis gone, along with my love. You and your saintly sinner are safe from me. I am come hither for my own, my two thousand pounds, and for nothing more."

"Ah! you are come back for money, not for me?" she murmured, with forced calmness.

"For money; and not for you, of course," said he, coldly.

The words wore hardly out of his month, when the proud lady flung his arm from her. "Then money shall you have, and not me; nor ought of me but my contempt."

But she could not carry it off as heretofore. She turned her back haughtily on him; but, at the first step, she burst out crying. "Come, and I'll give you what you are come for," she sobbed. "Ungrateful! heartless! Oh, how little I knew this man!"

She crept away before him, drooping her head, and crying bitterly; and he followed her, hanging his head, and ill at ease; for there was such true passion in her voice, her streaming eyes, and indeed in her whole body, that he was moved, and the part he was playing revolted him. He felt confused and troubled, and asked himself how on earth it was that she, the guilty one, contrived to appear the injured one, and made him, the wronged one, feel almost remorseful.

Mrs. Gaunt took no more notice of him now than if he had been a dog following at her heels. She went into the drawing-room, and sank helplessly on the nearest couch; threw her head wearily back, and shut her eyes. Yet the tears trickled through the closed lids.

Griffith caught up a hand-bell, and rang it vigorously.

Quick light steps were soon heard pattering; and in darted Caroline Ryder, with an anxious face; for of late she had conceived a certain sober regard for her mistress, who had ceased to be her successful rival, and who bore her grief like a man.

At sight of Griffith, Ryder screamed aloud, and stood panting.

Mrs. Gaunt opened her eyes. "Ay, child, he has come home," said she, bitterly; "his body, but not his heart."

She stretched her hand out feebly, and pointed to a bottle of salts that stood on the table. Ryder ran and put them to her nostrils. Mrs. Gaunt whispered in her ear, "Send a swift horse for Father Francis; tell him, life or death!"

Ryder gave her a very intelligent look, and presently slipped out, and ran into the stable-yard.

At the gate she caught sight of Griffith's horse. What does this quick-witted creature do but send the groom off on that horse, and not on Mrs. Gaunt's.

"Now, Dame," said Griffith, doggedly, "are you better?"

"Ay, I thank you."

"Then listen to me. When you and I set up house together, I had two thousand pounds. I spent it on this house. The house is yours. You told me so, one day, you know."

"Ah, you can remember my faults."

"I remember all, Kate."

"Thank you, at least, for calling me Kate. Well, Griffith, since you abandoned us, I thought, and thought, and thought, of all that might befall you; and I said, 'What will he do for money? My jewels, that you did me the honour to take, would not last you long, I feared. So I reduced my expenses three-fourths at least, and I put by some money for your need."

Griffith looked amazed. "For my need?" said he.

"For whose else? I'll send for it, and place it in your hands—to-morrow."

"To-morrow? Why not to-day?"

"I have a favour to ask of you first."

"What is that?"

"Justice. If you are fond of money, I too have something I prize: my honour. You have belied and insulted me, sir; but I know you were under a delusion. I mean to remove that delusion, and make you see how little I am to blame: for, alas! I own I was imprudent. But, oh Griffith! as I hope to be saved, it was the imprudence of innocence and over-confidence."

"Mistress," said Griffith, in a stern, yet agitated voice, "be advised, and leave all this: rouse not a man's sleeping wrath. Let bygones be bygones."

Mrs. Gaunt rose, and said, faintly, "So be it. I must go, sir, and give some orders for your entertainment."

"Oh; don't put yourself about for me," said Griffith, "I am not the master of this house."

Mrs. Gaunts lip trembled, but she was a match for him. "Then are you my guest," said she; "and my credit is concerned in your comfort."

She made him a curtsy, as if he were a stranger, and marched to the door, concealing, with great pride and art, a certain trembling of her knees.

At the door she found Ryder, and bade her follow, much to that lady's disappointment; for she desired a tête-à-tête with Griffith, and an explanation.

As soon as the two women were out of Griffith's hearing, the mistress laid her hand on the servant's arm, and, giving way to her feelings, said, all in a flutter, "Child, if I have been a good mistress to thee, show it now. Help me keep him in the house till Father Francis comes."

"I undertake to do so much," said Ryder, firmly. "Leave it to me, mistress."

Mrs. Gaunt threw her arms round Ryder's neck and kissed her.

It was done so ardently, and by a woman hitherto so dignified and proud, that Ryder was taken by surprise, and almost affected.

As for the service Mrs. Gaunt had asked of her, it suited her own designs.

"Mistress," said she, "be ruled by me; keep out of his way a-bit, while I get Miss Rose ready. You understand."

"Ah! I have one true friend in the house," said poor Mrs. Gaunt. She then confided in Ryder, and went away to give her own orders for Griffith's reception.

Ryder found little Rose, dressed her to perfection, and told her her dear papa was come home. She then worked upon the child's mind in that subtle way known to women, so that Rose went downstairs loaded and primed, though no distinct instructions had been given her.

As for Griffith, he walked up and down, uneasy; and wished he had stayed at the "Packhorse." He had not bargained for all these emotions; the peace of mind he had enjoyed for some months seemed trickling away.

"Mercy, my dear," said he, to himself, "'twill be a dear penny to me, I doubt."

Then he went to the window, and looked at the lawn, and sighed. Then he sat down, and thought of the past.

Whilst he sat thus moody, the door opened very softly, and a little cherubic face, with blue eyes and golden hair, peeped in. Griffith started. "Ah!" cried Rose, with a joyful scream: and out flew her little arms, and away she came, half running, half dancing, and was on his knee in a moment, with her arms round his neck.

"Papa! papa!" she cried. "Oh, my dear, dear, dear, darling papa!" And she kissed and patted his cheek again and again.

Her innocent endearments moved him to tears. "My pretty angel!" he sighed: "my lamb!"

"How your heart beats: don't cry, dear papa. Nobody is dead: only we thought you were. I'm so glad you are come home alive. Now we can take off this nasty black: I hate it."

"What, 'tis for me you wear it, pretty one?"

"Ay. Mamma made us. Poor mamma has been so unhappy. And that reminds me: you are a wicked man, papa. But I love you all one for that. It tis so dull when everybody is good like mamma; and she makes me dreadfully good too; but now you are come back, there will be a little, little, wickedness again, it is to be hoped. Aren't you glad you are not dead, and are come home instead? I am."

"I am glad I have seen thee. Come, take my hand, and let us go look at the old place."

"Ay. But you must wait till I get on my new hat and feather."

"Nay, nay; art pretty enough bareheaded."

"Oh, papa! but I must, for decency. You are company now, you know."

"Dull company, sweetheart, thou'lt find me."

"I don't mean that: I mean, when you were here always, you were only papa; but now you come once in an age, you're COMPANY. I won't budge without 'em; so there, now."

"Well, little one, I do submit to thy hat and feather: only be quick or I shall go forth without thee."

"If you dare," said Rose, impetuously: "for I won't be half a moment."

She ran and extorted from Ryder the new hat and feather, which by rights she was not to have worn until next month.

Griffith and his little girl went all over the well-known premises, he sad and moody, she excited and chattering, and nodding her head down, and cocking her eye up every now and then, to get a glimpse of her feather.

"And don't you go away again, dear papa. It tis so dull without you. Nobody comes here. Mamma won't let 'em."

"Nobody except Father Leonard," said Griffith, bitterly.

"Father Leonard? Why, he never comes here. Leonard! That is the beautiful priest that used to pat me on the head, and bid me love and honour my parents. And so I do. Only mamma is always crying, and you keep away: so how can I love and honour you, when I never see you, and they keep telling me you are good for nothing, and dead."

"My young mistress, when did you see Father Leonard last?" said Griffith, gnawing his lip.

"How can I tell? Why it was miles ago; when I was a mere girl. You know he went away before you did."

"I know nothing of the kind. Tell me the truth now. He has visited here since I went away."

"Nay, papa."

"That is strange. She visits him, then?"

"What, mamma? She seldom stirs out; and never beyond the village. We keep no carriage now. Mamma is turned such a miser. She is afraid you will be poor; so she puts it all by for you. But now you are come, we shall have carriages and things again. Oh, by-the-by, Father Leonard! I heard them say he had left England, so I did."

"When was that?"

"Well, I think that was a little bit after you went away."

"That is strange," said Griffith, thoughtfully.

He led his little girl by the hand, but scarcely listened to her prattle; he was so surprised and puzzled by the information he had elicited from her.

Upon the whole, however, he concluded that his wife and the priest had perhaps been smitten with remorse, and had parted,—when it was too late.

This, and the peace of mind he had found elsewhere, somewhat softened his feelings towards them. "So," thought he, "they were not hardened creatures after all. Poor Kate!"

As these milder feelings gained on him, Rose suddenly uttered a joyful cry; and, looking up, he saw Mrs. Gaunt coming towards him, and Ryder behind her. Both were in gay colours, which, in fact, was what had so delighted Rose.

They came up, and Mrs. Gaunt seemed a changed woman. She looked young and beautiful, and bent a look of angelic affection on her daughter; and said to Griffith, "Is she not grown? Is she not lovely? Sure you will never desert her again."

"'Twas not her I deserted, but her mother; and she had played me false with her d——d priest," was Griffith's reply.

Mrs. Gaunt drew back with horror. "This, before my girl?" she cried. "Griffith Gaunt, you lie!"

And this time it was the woman who menaced the man. She rose to six feet high, and advanced on him with her great grey eyes flashing flames at him. "Oh, that I were a man!" she cried: "this insult should be the last. I'd lay you dead at her feet and mine."

Griffith actually drew back a step; for the wrath of such a woman was terrible; more terrible perhaps to a brave man than to a coward.

Then he put his hands in his pockets with a dogged air; and said, grinding his teeth: "But—as you are not a man, and I'm not a woman, we can't settle it that way. So I give you the last word, and good day. I'm sore in want of money; but I find I can't pay the price it is like to cost me. Farewell."

"Begone!" said Mrs. Gaunt: "and, this time, for ever. Ruffian, and fool, I loathe the sight of you."

Rose ran weeping to her. "Oh, mamma, don't quarrel with papa:" then back to Griffith, "Oh, papa, don't quarrel with mamma—for my sake."

Griffith hung his head, and said, in a broken voice: "No, my lamb, we twain must not quarrel before thee. We will part in silence, as becomes those that once were dear, and have thee to show for't. Madam, I wish you all health and happiness. Adieu."

He turned on his heel; and Mrs. Gaunt took Rose to her knees, and bent and wept over her. Niobe over her last was not more graceful, nor more sad.

As for Ryder she stole quietly after her retiring master. She found him peering about, and asked him demurely what he was looking for.

"My good black horse, girl, to take me from this cursed place. Did I not tie him to your gate?"

"The black horse? Why I sent him for Father Francis. Nay, listen to me, master; you know I was always your friend, and hard upon her. Well, since you went, things have come to pass that make me doubt. I do begin to fear you were too hasty."

"Do you tell me this now, woman?" cried Griffith, furiously.

"How could I tell you before? Why did you break your tryst with me? If you had come according to your letter, I'd have told you months ago what I tell you now; but, as I was saying, the priest never came near her after you left; and she never stirred abroad to meet him. More than that, he has left England."

"Remorse! Too late."

"Perhaps it may, sir. I couldn't say; but there is one coming that knows the very truth."

"Who is that?"

"Father Francis. The moment you came, sir, I took it on me to send for him. You know the man: he won't tell a lie to please our Dame. And he knows all: for Leonard has confessed to him. I listened and heard him say as much. Then, master, be advised, and get the truth from Father Francis."

Griffith trembled. "Francis is an honest man," said he; "I'll wait till he comes. But oh, my lass, I find money may be bought too dear."

"Your chamber is ready, sir; and your clothes put out. Supper is ordered. Let me show you your room. We are all so happy now."

"Well," said he, listlessly, "since my horse is gone, and Francis coming, and I'm wearied and sick of the world, do what you will with me for this one day."

He followed her mechanically to a bedroom, where was a bright fire, and a fine shirt, and his silver-laced suit of clothes airing.

A sense of luxurious comfort struck him at the sight.

"Ay," he said, "I'll dress, and so to supper; I'm main hungry. It seems a man must eat, let his heart be ever so sore."

Before she left him, Ryder asked him coldly why he had broken his appointment with her.

"That is too long a story to tell you now," said he, coolly.

"Another time then," said she; and went out smiling, but bitter at heart.

Griffith had a good wash, and enjoyed certain little conveniences which he had not at the "Packhorse." He doffed his riding suit, and donned the magnificent dress Ryder had selected for him; and with his fine clothes he somehow put on more ceremonious manners.

He came down to the dining-room. To his surprise he found it illuminated with wax candles, and the table and sideboard gorgeous with plate.

Supper soon smoked upon the board; but, though it was set for three, nobody else appeared.

Griffith inquired of Ryder whether he was to sup alone.

She replied, "My mistress desires you not to wait for her. She has no stomach."

"Well, then, I have," said Griffith; and fell o with a will.

Ryder, who waited on this occasion, stood and eyed him with curiosity. His conduct was so unlike a woman's.

Just as he concluded, the door opened, and a burly form entered. Griffith rose and embraced him with his arms and lips, after the fashion of the day. "Welcome, thou one honest priest!" said he.

"Welcome, thrice welcome, my long-lost son!" said the cordial Francis.

"Sit down, man, and eat with me. I'll begin again, for you."

"Presently, Squire; I've work to do first. Go thou and bid thy mistress to come hither to me."

Ryder, to whom this was addressed, went out, and left the gentlemen together.

Father Francis drew out of his pocket two packets, carefully tied and sealed. He took a knife from the table and cut the strings, and broke the seals. Griffith eyed him with curiosity.

Father Francis looked at him. "These," said he, very gravely, "are the letters that Brother Leonard hath written, at sundry times, to Catherine Gaunt, and these are the letters Catherine Gaunt hath written to Brother Leonard."

Griffith trembled, and his face was convulsed.

"Let me read them at once," said he: and stretched out his hand, with eyes like a dog's in the dark.

Francis withdrew them, quietly. "Not till she is also present," said he.

At that Griffith's good-nature, multiplied by a good supper, took the alarm. "Come, come, sir," said he, "have a little mercy. I know you are a just man, and, though a boon companion, most severe in all matters of morality. But, I tell you plainly, if you are going to drag this poor woman in the dirt, I shall go out of the room. What is the use tormenting her? I've told her my mind before her own child: and now I wish I had not. When I caught them in the Grove I lifted my hand to strike her, and she never winced; I had better have left that alone too, methinks. D—n the women: you are always in the wrong if you treat 'em like men. They are not wicked; they are weak. And this one hath lain in my bosom, and borne me two children, and one he lieth in the churchyard, and t'other hath her hair and my very eyes: and the truth is, I can't bear any man on earth to miscall her but myself. God help me: I doubt I love her still too well to sit by and see her tortured. She was all in black for her fault, poor penitent wretch. Give me the letters; but let her be."

Francis was moved by this appeal, but shook his head solemnly; and, ere Griffith could renew his argument, the door was flung open by Ryder, and a stately figure sailed in that took both the gentlemen by surprise.

It was Mrs. Gaunt, in full dress. Rich brocade that swept the ground: magnificent bust, like Parian marble varnished; and on her brow a diadem of emeralds and diamonds that gave her beauty an imperial stamp.

She swept into the room as only fine women can sweep, made Griffith a haughty curtsy, and suddenly lowered her head, and received Father Francis's blessing: then seated herself, and quietly awaited events.

"The brazen jade!" thought Griffith. "But how divinely beautiful!" And he became as agitated as she was calm—in appearance. For, need I say her calmness was put on? Defensive armour made for her by her pride and her sex.

The voice of Father Francis now rose, solid, grave, and too impressive to be interrupted.

"My daughter, and you who are her husband and my friend, I am here to do justice between you both, with God's help; and to show you both your faults.

"Catherine Gaunt, you began the mischief, by encouraging; another man to interfere between you and your husband in things secular."

"But, father, he was my director, my priest."

"My daughter, do you believe, with the Protestants, that marriage is a mere civil contract; or do you hold, with us, that it is one of the holy sacraments?"

"Can you ask me?" murmured Kate, reproachfully.

"Well, then, those whom God and the whole Church have in holy sacrament united, what right hath a single priest to disunite in heart, and make the wife false to any part whatever of that most holy vow? I hear, and not from you, that Leonard did set you against your husband's friends, withdrew you from society, and sent him abroad alone. In one word, he robbed your husband of his companion and his friend. The sin was Leonard's: but the fault was yours. You were five years older than Leonard, and a woman of sense and experience; he but a boy by comparison. What right had you to surrender your understanding, in a matter of this kind, to a poor silly priest, fresh from his seminary, and as manifestly without a grain of common sense as he was full of piety?"

This remonstrance produced rather a striking effect on both those who heard it. Mrs. Gaunt seemed much struck with it. She leaned back in her chair, and put her hand to her brow with a sort of despairing gesture that Griffith could not very well understand: it seemed to him so disproportionate.

It softened him, however, and he faltered out, "Ay, father, that is how it all began. Would to heaven it had stopped there."

Francis resumed. "This false step led to consequences you never dreamed of; for one of your romantic notions is, that a priest is an angel. I have known you, in former times, try to take me for an angel: then would I throw cold water on your folly by calling lustily for chines of beef and mugs of ale. But I suppose Leonard thought himself an angel too; and the upshot was, he fell in love with his neighbour's wife."

"And she with him," groaned Griffith.

"Not so," said Francis; "but perhaps she was nearer it than she thinks."

"Prove that," said Mrs. Gaunt, "and I'll fall on my knees to him before you."

Francis smiled, and proceeded. "To be sure, from the moment you discovered Leonard was in love with you, you drew back, and conducted yourself with prudence and propriety. Read these letters, sir, and tell me what you think of them."

He handed them to Griffith. Griffith's hand trembled visibly as he took them.

"Stay," said Father Francis; "your better way will be to read the whole correspondence according to their dates. Begin with this of Mrs. Gaunt's."

Griffith read the letter in an audible whisper.

Mrs. Gaunt turned her head a little, and for the first time lowered her eyes to the ground.